VELMA

Jinkies! It doesn't seem that long ago.

My friends and I had some wild times back in high school. That's when we became Mystery, Inc. and spent all our time solving mind-boggling mysteries.

Our personalities were very different, but together we made an unstoppable team. My role was clear enough. I was the brainy girl, the smart one.

That was okay with me. I never cared too much about fashion and being popular. I guess no one would have ever called me pretty. But I didn't care. Nothing made me happier than uncovering a clue that would help unravel a mystery.

I never got enough credit for it, though. At least that was how it seemed to me. Even though

I came up with all the fascinating facts and unfathomable figures, Fred always acted like *he* had figured it all out. He was the leader, the one who made the final plan.

It drove me crazy!

Without me, Fred would have been lucky to solve the mystery of how to tie his shoes! I guess it was because he was a guy, the coolest kid at Coolsville High. He honestly believed that because he was the star of the football team and all the girls loved him that he deserved all the credit for the cases we solved.

Fred always drove the Mystery Machine, our van. Every single time, Fred directed who would go where and do what. And he absolutely *always*, one hundred percent of the time, made sure that when we split up, he was with Daphne.

Why shouldn't he? Daphne was rich and cute, just the kind of girl Fred liked.

I didn't blame Daphne. She was nice enough and she tried hard. But somehow she was always getting caught or captured — the classic damsel in distress. I didn't mind that much because finding Daphne and saving her was part of the fun.

Of course, there were also Shaggy and Scooby-Doo. I don't know exactly how to describe *them*. They were pretty unique.

Scooby was a giant Great Dane who sometimes seemed more like a person than a dog. When he barked, it actually sounded like he was saying something.

And — come to think of it — Scooby's owner, Shaggy, often seemed more like a dog than a person. He was fun and agreeable, but also very goofy.

Scooby and Shaggy had a lot in common. For one thing, they loved to eat. I mean they adored it. Jinkies! They'd do almost anything for food — especially for their favorite, Scooby Snacks.

Neither of them was particularly brave, either. As soon as the bad guy showed up you'd hear their six feet scuffling across the floor as they ran away. But when it was time to lure the villain out into the open, they could be counted on to help — especially if you had a box of Scooby Snacks to bribe them with.

For a while, everything was perfect. We were the best of friends. We didn't even mind being smooshed together in the front seat of the Mystery Machine, the van Daphne's dad gave us.

But little by little, we began annoying one another. I wanted more credit for the work I did. I was also getting tired of saving Daphne. It just wasn't fun anymore. I began to resent all the time we had to spend saving her. (And secretly, I began wondering why they couldn't save *me* once in a while.)

Even Fred was starting to get tired of it. That was probably because *he* wanted to get kidnapped. He wanted *everything* to revolve around him. Fred's ego totally took over.

Even Daphne was getting tired of being captured. She wanted us to see that there was more to her than just a pretty face. She couldn't tell us what more there was, though, because she didn't know herself.

We'd just solved a big case on the day we decided to split up. I was feeling really crabby and unappreciated. Especially since Fred had just taken the credit for one of my plans — AGAIN. I'd had enough of that, and I told him so.

"Some plan," Daphne said sarcastically. "That ghost breathed his nasty halitosis-breath on me for an hour and a half."

"It's not our fault you always get kidnapped," I replied, rolling my eyes.

"I can't believe you'd say that to me," Daphne said, looking hurt.

Fred sighed, "Listen, our roles have been foisted upon us. I'm the front man, I deal with the public. Velma, you're a behind-the-scenes type of gal. And Daph, you're pretty, but helpless."

Daphne was really steamed now. "Pretty, yes, but not helpless!"

I snorted. "Please. You come with your own ransom note."

Before I could stop her, Daphne reached out and grabbed my glasses.

"Who's helpless now?"

I was totally blind.

"I'm going to kill you, Daphne," I shouted. I snatched my glasses back. "That's it, I quit!"

"No way!" Daphne shouted.

For a moment, I thought she didn't want me to go. I was touched. But then she continued. "You can't quit! I was going to quit in two seconds. Now everyone is going to think I copied off the smart girl!"

Fred looked thoughtful. "Maybe *I* quit." He wasn't exactly sure, but he was obviously considering the idea. "I *do*! I do quit!"

I hadn't really wanted to break up the group. Deep down, I think I only wanted them to assure me that I was appreciated. Instead, I'd started a trend — a quitting trend.

Suddenly it all became clear to me. Fred and

Daphne were so self-centered! They only cared about themselves.

Shaggy and Scooby were sweet enough. They stood there looking confused, like they couldn't figure out what was going on. But the other two — I never wanted to see them again!

"I'm out of here!" I shouted as I stormed away from them.

SHAGGY

Zoinks! I never thought it could happen. Like, I thought my pals and I would solve mysteries 2gether 4ever. Then Mystery, Inc. broke up and it was just Scoob and me.

We were sad at first. But we made the best of it. We drove the Mystery Machine as far as it would go. We ended up in a way-cool place by the ocean. We couldn't eat the sand-which-is-there. (Get it?) So we used the sand to make flower-pots, which we sold.

Before long, we had a pretty sweet life going. We were living in the Mystery Machine, making pots, and groovin' to the beat of the ocean waves. We hadn't solved a mystery in a way-long time.

Then one day Scooby and I were in the van eating one of our favorite dishes — chocolate-covered eggplant burgers — when someone knocked. I slid the door open and laid my eyes on a wild-looking character. Half of him was official-looking in a business suit. The other half was wild native style. Feathers and native grass stuck out of his suit. He wore beads and shells in his crazy hair.

He handed me an envelope addressed to NORVILLE "SHAGGY" ROGERS AND SCOOBERT-DOO, CORNER OF 5TH AND OCEAN, USA. "I'm looking for Mr. Rogers and Mr. Doo — the detectives?" he said.

I didn't like the sound of it. In fact, I totally freaked.

He called us detectives! That meant someone wanted us to solve a case.

No way!

Scoob and I liked the peaceful life we'd had since leaving Mystery, Inc. I didn't miss being scared out of my wits by ghosts and goblins, even if they did always turn out to be guys in masks. There was no way I wanted to start *that* again.

I handed the envelope back to the freaky guy. Then I turned to Scooby. "Like, grab the food and let's scram-o!"

Scoob and I scooped up our chocolate-covered eggplant burgers and crashed out the van door to get away from the guy. "Look, you look like a very nice freakish dude," I said, "but we aren't detectives anymore."

The dude waved his envelope. "Wait, please. I have been sent by my employer, Mr. Emile Mondavarious, to invite you to his world-famous amusement park, Spooky Island."

"Man, we don't go near any place with *spooky*, *haunted*, *forbidden*, or *creepy* in the name," I informed him. I backed away with Scooby at my side.

"But the esteemed Mr. Mondavarious would like you to solve a mystery!" he said.

"Sorry, dude," I replied, "but us and mysteries go together like bad seafood and weak stomachs — one taste and we can't stop running."

"But Mr. Mondavarious will pay you a fee of ten thousand American dollars," the dude added.

I waved him off as Scoob and I started walking away. "Materialism's, like, not our bag," I said.

He followed us. "He will provide you with free airfare!"

"No way!" I shouted, walking faster.

"Room and board," he tried.

"Nuh-uh," I said.

"And all you can eat!"

Scoob and I both stopped short.

We looked at each other. Slowly we both grinned. This dude was finally talking our language. "Lead the way, my man," I told him.

A long white limousine slid up alongside us at the curb. "Right this way," he said, opening the back door.

We got in and found a big bowl of ice-cold shrimp waiting for us. This idea seemed tastier every second. We were so busy eating, we hardly noticed as the limo pulled into the airport parking lot.

The next thing we knew, we were walking through the airport, headed for someplace called Spooky Island. I tried to think of it as Yummy Island.

I was lost in an "all you can eat" daydream when I noticed someone moving across the airport lobby. That someone looked very familiar.

FRED

I hadn't gone halfway across the lobby of the airport before I was spotted. Three young women — obviously fans — looked at me and began to shout.

"He's so cute!"

"Oh, my god! It's him!"

"Adorable!"

They raced toward me. I took a pen from my pocket, preparing to sign their autographs. As usual, I'd protest a little, then give in. It made the autograph more special for them if they believed they'd cajoled me into it.

When they were just a few feet away, I spoke to them. "Sorry, girls. No time for autographs. I've got a plane to . . ."

My sentence hung in midair. I couldn't believe it. They hadn't even glanced in my direction as they ran past me. Looking to see where they'd gone, I found them making a fuss over a woman holding a small baby.

Outshone by a drooling infant! This was not a good sign.

I sighed and finally realized that I had to face the fact I'd been denying for so long. I was losing my fan base. Fred Jones was no longer the hot property he'd been a mere six months ago. It wouldn't be long before I became a total has-been.

I was jolted from these depressing thoughts by a tap on my shoulder. I turned and — looking down — saw someone I'd thought I'd never see again.

"Velma!" I shouted.

"Hi, Fred," she said. She hadn't changed much — actually, not at all.

She wore her trademark outfit, an orange turtleneck sweater with matching orange knee-socks. Her orange suit and oversized glasses were just as I remembered. Even her pageboy haircut was the same.

We shared an awkward moment before I could think of something to say. "You're going this way?" I asked.

She nodded. Another uncomfortable moment passed. I really had no idea what to say to her.

The last time we'd spoken, we'd both been very angry. But I didn't feel angry with her now. Too much time had passed. She didn't seem angry with me, either.

We smiled nervously at each other and began walking side by side. "So, how have you been?" she asked.

"Great," I told her. "I've been on a lecture tour with my new book, *Fred on Fred: The Many Faces of Myself.*"

I just happened to have a copy in my carry-on bag so I pulled it out to show her. I took a moment to glance at the cover. I never tire of looking at it. It features a large picture of me, with another picture of me in the background.

Fred on Fred is a collection of my many mystery-solving adventures as the leader of Mystery, Inc. I'd been traveling around the country speaking about my creative solutions to solving these mysteries in front of enthralled, love-crazed (mostly female) audiences.

"A book tour! Jinkies, that's impressive!" Velma said. Was that a trace of jealousy in her voice?

"And yourself?" I inquired, to be polite.

"I've been working at NASA, designing hydro-powered missile defense systems," she replied.

Poor Velma, I thought. She'd never had anything going for her other than awesome intelligence. Since there was little else she could do, she obviously had no career choice besides brain work.

"I've also been on a journey of self-discovery," she added.

The self-discovery thing didn't seem too interesting, so I figured the polite approach was to talk about NASA. "NASA, huh?" I said, trying to look interested. "That's the company that created Pokémon, right? Which one's your favorite? I like that duck that shoots rays."

Velma shot me a look I didn't understand. I decided it was probably just her way of expressing admiration for the way I can speak knowledgeably about many subjects.

We arrived at my gate and I stopped. Velma stopped, too.

"Is this your gate?" we both asked at the same time.

We checked each other's boarding passes. We were on the same flight!

And then, from behind me, I heard a familiar voice.

"What do you mean, I have too many carry-on bags?"

DAPHNE

As if things weren't bad enough! The airline was being so mean! They wouldn't let me bring my bags on the plane. Then I looked over and saw Fred Jones hurrying toward me. Of all the people I did not want to see!

And then it got worse.

Velma Dinkley was with him!

I shooed them away. "Oh, no! I'm not talking to you guys anymore!" I zipped my lip to make my feelings as clear as possible.

They just stood there and stared at me. Unfortunately, my detective's curiosity overcame my common sense and I just had to ask. "What the heck are you two doing here?"

"I'm guessing we all received the same letter from the owner of Spooky Island. He requested our help in solving a mystery," Velma said.

We all looked at one another for a moment. It was true. I'd received a letter exactly like the one Velma described. I'd thought the letter had come only to me. But, obviously, I was wrong.

Suddenly, I was so mad! I didn't care who was watching. I stamped my feet on the ground as hard as I could. "That's not fair!" I shouted. "I was going to solve a mystery all by myself for the first time ever!"

Fred stifled a snicker. "How were you going to save yourself when you got caught?"

I wanted to hurt him. Bad! I could have, too. "I'm not like that anymore," I informed him. "I've transformed my body into a dangerous weapon!"

Both of them bit their lips, looking like they were about to break into hysterical laughter.

Let them laugh, I thought. My karate instructor had laughed, too. But I knew I was developing into a truly awesome martial artist, even if it didn't exactly show . . . yet.

My opponent is my insecurity, I reminded myself. *My strength is my resolve.* I summoned my *chi*, my inner strength. I was going to need it to deal with these two again.

"Who's this Emile Mondavarious who wants us all together?" Fred questioned.

Velma sighed. I'd heard that sigh a million times. She always sighed like that when she was about to imply that Fred and I were just the two biggest dumbbells on the planet. "You guys never do the research," she began. "He's a mysterious recluse obsessed with horror movies and amusement park rides."

I was about to tell her not to be such a know-it-all, but I became distracted by another familiar face coming toward us.

"Far-out! I guess we're all going to Spooky Island."

"Shaggy!" I cried. He was the only one of the old gang I was actually happy to see.

"Et tu, Shagopolis?" Fred said, probably trying to sound smart.

"Where's Scooby?" Velma asked.

Shaggy jerked his thumb over his shoulder. "They, like, don't allow dogs over fifteen pounds on the plane, so we made, like, sort of a plan."

I gazed over his shoulder in the direction he'd indicated — and gasped with horror. "Oh. My. God!" I said. I could *not* believe what was headed toward us.

Scooby-Doo staggered forward, stumbling in high heels. And it didn't stop with the heels.

There was also a gray wig, a floral-patterned dress, a floppy bonnet, and a pair of rhinestone-studded glasses. Plus, he was wearing a hideous amount of red lipstick.

"You've got to be kidding!" Velma said, staring at Scooby.

"No one is stupid enough to believe that," I told Shaggy.

Fred leaned in toward Shaggy. "Who's the ugly old broad?" he whispered to Shaggy.

Well, almost no one.

An announcement came over the loudspeaker. "Flight 3774 to Spooky Island, now boarding."

We all looked at one another, uncertain if we wanted to do this. "You know," Fred said, "a Mystery, Inc. reunion could be a publicity bonanza for me."

That made me mad. "You only want publicity so you can be in magazines and people will hear about you."

"That's what publicity is," he said in that smug voice I knew so well.

"I'm not getting back together just so you can have your calls returned by the Harlem Globetrotters," I snapped. We'd solved a great mystery with their help. But Fred was so conceited now I bet the Globetrotters didn't want to know him anymore.

"But it's not too late now, right?" Shaggy said. "Mystery, Inc., together again like a Marky Mark and the Funky Bunch reunion, only instead of Marky Mark and the Funky Bunch, there's us. Let's do that thing where we, like, put our hands on top of one another, then lift them up and go, 'Whoo-hoo!'"

"Rokay!" Scooby agreed. He put his paw on Shaggy's hand and lifted it up. "Roo-hoo!" he cried.

"Wait for everybody, Scoob," Shaggy told him. He looked at the three of us with pleading eyes.

I could see he wanted us all to be a team again. I wasn't sure I was ready for this, though. "Only if Fred and Velma do it," I gave in.

"People are watching, Shag," Fred said, shaking his head. He and Velma just turned and headed for the boarding gate.

Well, if that was the way they wanted to be, I could be just the same. I headed for the boarding gate, too.

"Roo-hoo," Scooby and Shaggy said sadly behind me.

I handed the attendant my ticket. While she stapled all the pieces together, I made a decision.

I'd be the leader on this case. They'd all see the new me. And — no matter what — I would *not* get kidnapped.

SHAGGY

Okay, like, so the old Mystery, Inc. gang wasn't what it used to be. Scooby and I were still glad to see them, though. For one thing, it meant we wouldn't be the only ones on Spooky Island.

As it turned out, there were a lot of people going to Spooky Island. The plane was packed, mostly with college kids.

Scooby's disguise fooled everyone. People who saw him instantly turned away, probably because they didn't want to stare. We sat together, about to enjoy a delicious airline sandwich. But I froze midbite, my mouth wide open.

How could I chew when the most beautiful woman in the entire world was walking right toward me?

"Excuse me. Excuse me," she said, making her way down the aisle.

Not only was she beautiful, with mustard-blond hair, smoothie-smooth skin, blueberry-blue eyes, and Jell-O red lips — but she seemed to have an inner glow, as if she drank sunshine (or, at the very least, Sunny De-Lite) for breakfast. Her long, rigatoni curls tumbled around her shoulders like a halo of pasta.

Then to my, like, stunned amazement, she stopped — right next to me!

I had a vague idea that Scooby was eating the sandwich I still held in my hand — but I couldn't even move to stop him. I wasn't able to take my eyes off this radiant goddess standing beside me.

She actually spoke to me! "Would you mind if I took the seat there next to, uh . . ."

Like, zoinks! She was pointing to the seat next to Scooby! "The seat next to my grandma? Like, no. I don't mind at all!"

What great luck! It was, like, fate. This was the girl I'd been waiting for, dreaming of, hungering for all my life.

She sank into her seat and sneezed. Then she sneezed again. "Wow! I'm sorry. My allergies are . . ." She stopped to sneeze another time. "It's usually only dogs that do it." She sneezed two more times, then stood. "Maybe I'd better move." She looked around the plane. "There's a seat in the back."

I couldn't let her go! I had to think of something.

Her eyes widened. "Hey, is that *Fred Jones* back there?"

Oh, no! Not Fred. If she sat by Fred I'd never see her again. He'd zero right in on her and turn on the charm. I wouldn't stand a chance then.

She stared at Fred. "When I was in high school I had a puffy sticker with his face on it," she told me dreamily.

"Yeah, he was a little puffier back then," I grumbled. Fred was no longer built like the quarterback he'd been in high school. But the girls still liked him just the same.

My chances were crumbling by the second. I couldn't let her leave her seat. "Listen," I said, "you're probably just allergic to Grandma's perfume. I mean, it even gets to me." I faked a sneeze to make my point. "See?"

I turned to Scooby. "Uh, Grandma, didn't you want to catch up with your old pal Velma back there? Huh?"

Scooby frowned at me. He knew I wanted him to leave, but I could tell his feelings were hurt. It wasn't like I was asking him for such a huge favor. It was a little thing to do for a pal.

"Rokay," he gave in gloomily. He stood and headed toward the back of the plane.

"That's better," my goddess said. "I'm Mary Jane."

What a delicious name! "Shaggy. Shaggy Rogers."

She began digging in her purse and pulled out a treasure beyond measure.

A box of Scooby Snacks!

I had to be dreaming! This girl was more than perfect! She was mega-perfecto! I kept staring at the box, not believing what I was seeing.

"They're for dogs, okay, I know," she said, sounding slightly embarrassed. "But they're a hundred percent vegetarian." She leaned in close and whispered, "And I love 'em."

My throat was dry as cotton candy but I had to force myself to speak. "Like, me too," I croaked.

"Far-out!" Mary Jane cheered, smiling with delight. "I've never met another person who —"

"Me neither!" I said dreamily.

This was going to be the best trip of my life — All-You-Can-Eat Island and Mary Jane. Zoinks! What could be better?

VELMA

Jinkies! What could be worse than spending hours on a plane with the biggest egomaniac on the planet, Fred Jones, and a giant Great Dane dressed as a grandmother and reeking of cheap perfume? Especially when Scooby started barking at this girl's cat. Fred started lecturing me on behavior modification for dogs, but when he tried demonstrating on Scooby, Scooby punched him in the nose. It was so embarrassing.

Daphne was no help. She had some big guy leaning on her shoulder, snoring in her ear. She just stared out the window as if she were in a world all her own. I wondered what she was thinking about.

Shaggy stayed up front. He seemed to be hypnotized by the hippie girl who'd plunked herself down beside him. I'd never seen him look so in love. Well, maybe once — when he got to eat twelve pizzas by himself. But I'd thought he was incapable of any romantic feelings beyond the ones he had for food.

Finally, I saw Spooky Island from my window as our plane descended. It was built on a large mountain. Dark clouds circled the mountaintop. The amusement park was nestled into some craggy cliffs.

The moment we walked off the plane, the weirdness began. A giant, terrifying statue with flashing eyes stood on the airfield. It gazed down on us. It must have been a carving of some island demon.

And then it began to talk in a booming voice!

"Welcome to Spooky Island — one of the top-five spring break vacation spots for college students." Scary music came out of the statue.

The statue was the only one there to greet us. There was no one else around anywhere.

"What happened to your new girlfriend?" I asked Shaggy as we walked across the airfield.

For the first time in my life, I saw Shaggy blush. "She said she needed to go find a friend. I'm sure I'll, like, see her later."

From the airport, we all followed signs pointing down to the shore. We had to drag Daphne's many suitcases along with us. A big, flat barge was there waiting at a dock. A sign on it read BARGE TO SPOOKY ISLAND AMUSEMENT PARK, so we boarded.

The college students didn't seem creeped out by any of this. They were here to be scared and thought it was a blast. I wasn't so sure that this was all in fun, though. It seemed awfully strange to me — and I'd been in some pretty peculiar places.

The boat crossed the water and pulled into a dock by a rickety amusement park pier. Another island demon statue like the one at the airport stood on the dock.

We were the last to get off because of all Daphne's luggage. We were pushing, pulling, and tugging it along the dock when a blast of dark smoke blew from the top of the demon statue's nose.

Scooby, Shaggy, Daphne, Fred, and I jumped back as the statue's arms suddenly jerked high up above its head and it spoke. "You're presently disembarking the *Barge of the Damned*. It's the only way on or off the island. Now your souls are trapped in a world of unrelenting horror!" Evil laughter rose from the statue.

The college students laughed as they walked by the statue.

"This statue might be a clue," I suggested. "Let's check it out."

The gang and I began circling it, searching for anything suspicious. Suddenly, I heard a sound. It was coming from inside the statue. "Shhh!" I told the others. I leaned in and rested my ear on the statue.

"Mystery, Inc.?" it whispered.

"We're here," I whispered back.

"You've made it!" the statue said, loudly this time. "This is wonderful! Hold on, let me remove myself." The statue began turning on its base. Its giant arms swung with each movement, and we had to leap out of the way to avoid being hit. One of the arms smacked into a passing college student. "So sorry," the voice inside the statue apologized.

In the next second a man's arm emerged from an opening in the side of the statue. "Could I trouble you for a hand?" he requested.

Shaggy grasped his wiggling fingers and pulled him all the way out of the statue. He was a thin, middle-aged man with dark hair.

He studied the statue critically. "It's a new exhibit. I haven't quite perfected it yet." Then he turned and looked us over. "Welcome," he said, spreading his arms in a friendly, embracing gesture. "I'm Emile Mondavarious, the owner of the amusement park."

"You?" I blurted.

"Yes."

He didn't fit my image of what a mysterious recluse millionaire would look like. He seemed much too ordinary for that. "You seem much less . . ." I began, but I didn't know how to finish without being rude.

"Spooky?" Mondavarious supplied the word.

"Yes," I agreed, "less spooky than we would have guessed."

"Oh, no, I can be very spooky," he insisted. "If called upon, I can be quite frightening." He struck some monstrous poses with his teeth bared and his fingers spread like claws. He growled and moved among us, leering. It was impressive.

"So you're the one who brought us here," I said.

He straightened, no longer being spooky. "No. What brought you here was your insatiable desire to be part of a juicy mystery."

Mondavarious snapped his fingers, and several very scary-looking face-painted helpers ran up to the dock. They wore a strange mishmash of outfits — grass skirts, skull chains, ripped T-shirts, and plastic leis. They grabbed Daphne's suitcases and scurried up the hill with them.

Daphne watched her suitcases go, then stepped closer to Mondavarious. "The truth is, Mr. Mondavarious, Mystery, Inc. has broken up."

"That's all right," Mondavarious replied. "Something broken up can be fixed — therein lies its potential. And I need you to fix Spooky Island."

"What's the problem, exactly?" I asked. "Ghost? Ogre? Zombie? Devil?" As I spoke, I saw Scooby and Shaggy shiver and move closer together.

"Heavens, no!" Mr. Mondavarous cried. "If I had one of those, I'd offer it a contract."

He lowered his voice and spoke in a confidential whisper. "I'm talking about something far worse, something intangible — possession!"

"There's no such thing as possession, or any other supernatural phenomena," Fred said.

"Except the proven entities, right?" asked Shaggy.

"Such as?" said Fred skeptically.

"Leprechauns, walking skeletons," Shaggy began.

"Rankenrerry!" Scooby put in.

"Right, Fr — no, Scooby," Shaggy said. "Frank-enberry is a guy on a cereal box." But suddenly, he looked scared, too. "Isn't he?"

Mondavarious led us through the entrance to the park. "Now, listen, and look around. Do you notice a difference between those coming and going?"

I looked at the kids around us. The people entering with us were all very different from one another — geebs, preps, goth kids, every kind of kid you can imagine. But all the people leaving were like cookie-cutter hipsters — they all looked exactly the same!

"The ones leaving all shop at the Gap?" Daphne asked.

"They look sort of alike," I agreed.

"Precisely," said Mondavarious. "And they didn't before they came! They've changed! In other words — *possession!*"

"What kind of possession?" I asked.

"The worst kind of possession — possession of the soul!" Mondavarious began. "Ten years ago I created Spooky Island as a place where young people could escape their humdrum suburban existence and experience a mix of fear and magic of world-transforming power."

I doubted there could be anything world-transforming about an amusement park, but I kept listening.

"Something supernatural has threatened all that," Mondavarious continued. "I'm terrified. I'll admit it. And the young people that come off that barge — the people I love the most — they're in danger."

We all took a step closer to Mondavarious, fascinated to hear this story. I, for one, was totally intrigued by this new case.

Mondavarious went on. "I don't know anything about mysteries. I devise loop-de-loops in the shape of skulls, Ferris wheels from animal bones. Now, however you feel about one another, I think you're heroes. Please! I beg you! Will you investigate?"

We looked at one another, still unsure. Daphne was the first one to speak. "I guess we could . . . see what we could do."

Mondavarious's thin face lit up with happiness. "Oh, thank you! Thank you! Oh, this is marvelous!" he cried. "Maybe we'll celebrate later by having a little Spookapalooza. Ha! We'll meet you tonight at the hotel, where you can regale me with stories of your past conquests." He began to hurry up the hill. "Farewell."

"Rye-rye, Rondavarious," Scooby said, waving.

I watched him go. There was something strange about that skinny little man. As he departed, he scratched his head, and he reminded me somehow of a dog.

Two people came down the hill, passing Mondavarious. As they got closer I could see them more clearly. "Jinkies!" I murmured. "What a strange-looking guy."

FRED

I looked up the hill and caught sight of a pretty bizarre-looking guy dressed all in black leather. Metal studs covered the leather. He had spiky jet-black hair. It was kind of a goth thing. He sure had a style sense of his own.

The woman beside him was petite and cute, not weird-looking like her friend. They stopped and seemed to argue about something. They were too far away for me to hear, but I could tell the woman was angry — really furious. The poor guy just seemed puzzled by her behavior. I wondered what he'd done to make her so mad.

I didn't think much of it other than to wonder how I could make points with the girl. Sure, Daphne had once been my number-one gal, but that was over now. I had to move on, and a guy who looked like that wouldn't be able to hang on to this cutie for long. Besides, she was already mad at him. But then something truly strange happened.

The woman lifted the guy into the air. High! And she held him straight over her head. She shook him as though he were lighter than a rag doll, then slammed him down on the ground.

The woman stormed off without looking back. We ran up to the guy to see what had happened. Shaggy crouched down beside him. "Are you, like, okay, dude?"

He slowly got up and rubbed his spiky head, flattening out a few of the spikes. "I have no idea," he admitted. "I've known Carol since we were two. Suddenly she's acting like I'm a stranger. And she was never that strong before."

He got to his feet and straightened his black fingerless gloves. "I'm Brad, but you can call me Brad the Goth. Everyone does."

I wondered about the scene I'd just witnessed. Mondavarious had mentioned possession. It seemed ridiculous. I always take the logical approach. Behind all of these so-called mysterious events is just a man in a mask and some kind of fancy equipment. My years of skillful sleuthing as the leader of Mystery, Inc. had certainly taught me that much.

Still, what I'd just seen was very strange. Something peculiar was certainly going on here. Once again I felt bitten by that old, familiar mystery-solving bug.

"I'm going to solve this one first," Velma announced.

Was she challenging my leadership? Apparently. "Not before I solve it first," I shot back.

"You guys will look like total, total idiots when you're kidnapped and I'm the one saving you!" Daphne said.

If that was the way they wanted it, I could more than meet their challenge. The race was on!

SHAGGY

Scoob and I really didn't care who solved the mystery first — as long as it wasn't us. I mean — zoinks! — who wants to be the first one to come across some ghoulish ghost or beastly beastie? Not us. We'd much rather sit back and enjoy some Scooby Snacks.

Still, we figured we'd do our share and poke around the pier searching for clues. As we walked along the water's edge, I thought I heard clamshells knocking together. "Hey, Scoob, clams on the half shell," I said. "Until the all-we-can-eat thing kicks in, how about a snack?"

When Scooby didn't reply, I turned to see what was up with him. He couldn't answer because his teeth were chattering too hard.

"Are you cold, pal?" I asked.

"Ro," he managed to say. "Rared."

"Scared, huh?" I said. "Well, it is, like, spooky

on Spooky Island. But you have to admit there's one pretty great girl right here."

The moment I said that — there she was. Mary Jane was standing on the dock. The setting sun bathed her in a glow like honey. It was a beautiful sight. She seemed to be searching for someone. When she saw me, she waved.

"Like, hi," I said, joining her on the dock.

"Like, hi," she replied. "I was supposed to meet my friend Bethanne here."

I checked around. There was no one else nearby.

Mary Jane giggled lightly. "If I know her, I'll find her at the snack bar."

"That just so happens to be where Scoob and I were about to search for clues," I fibbed.

"Ro rit's rot," Scooby corrected me.

"It is now," I whispered to him.

"Great, let's go!" Mary Jane said. "The bar is in the hotel just up the hill." She began walking up the hill and I hurried to keep up with her. She walked fast. I didn't mind, though. With my angel-hair-pasta girl beside me, I was flying on the wings of love.

DAPHNE

I was determined to solve this case first. That meant I couldn't waste a minute. I headed right to the park's boardwalk to search for clues.

It was a really creepy place. The rides had names like BOTCHED SURGERY WATER SLIDE, BOATING FATALITY BUMPER BOATS, and DEN OF BRUISES.

In a dark corner, beside a game stall, I saw an amazing-looking guy. His long black hair hung around his shoulders. He wore ripped pants and a hideous old jacket with no shirt underneath.

Two college guys passed me. I noticed one held a brown paper bag. "Hey, look! It's the Voodoo Maestro," one whispered to the other, pointing to the weird guy.

They approached him and quickly handed him the bag. He paid them money and then they hurried away.

My finely tuned detective antennae went up. This was the kind of suspicious behavior and creepy character that always led to a clue. I'd hang back, then follow him to see where he went.

I ducked into a space between the game stalls and peered out, waiting for the Voodoo Maestro to make his move.

Someone grabbed my arm. I jumped, ready to use my karate skills.

But it was only Fred. "Hey, Daph," he said.

"What are you doing here? I thought we were working separately!" I said, annoyed.

"Separately together," he said with a dumb grin. "Kinda reminds you of old times, doesn't it?"

I snorted disgustedly. "Like when you played around on me with all those fans. You were like a lion with impalas, looking for the ones who were wounded or too young to know any better."

As I spoke to him, I kept my eyes on the Voodoo Maestro. He had moved off the board-walk and was heading toward a wooded area.

"Daphne, just exactly what are you implying about me and impalas?" Fred questioned.

He could be such an idiot! I don't know what I had ever liked about him. "Just leave me alone, Fred," I snapped.

I had no more time for this stupid conversation. My suspect was getting away from me. Leaving Fred behind, I headed toward the wooded area where palm trees and tropical plants stood in a thick tangle. That's where the Voodoo Maestro had gone.

I caught sight of him up ahead. It was sunset and would soon be completely dark. I didn't like the idea of being out here in these spooky woods at night. But a detective can't give in to fear. I kept moving forward through the woods like a ninja warrior.

In another fifteen minutes, the Voodoo Maestro stepped into a clearing in the woods. He headed for a tiny wooden shack.

I crouched behind some tropical ferns, watching, not sure exactly what to do next. What if he didn't return?

If he didn't come out — I'd have to go in.

I shivered. No way was I going in there by myself.

But I had to go. I'd worked too hard on not being a wimpy, girlie-girl damsel in distress. I was now a strong, new, brave me! What was there to be afraid of? After all, I had my looks, my charm, my karate skills.

I walked toward the shack and pushed in the

wooden door. It was unlocked. The room was all shadowy darkness and I couldn't see anything at first. As my eyes adjusted, though, I saw a very strange sight.

The Voodoo Maestro sat cross-legged on the floor. In front of him was a wrapped, store-bought chicken. An empty paper bag lay in the corner. It was the same bag the college students had handed him. They must have bought the chicken for him.

The packaged chicken dangled there, hanging from a string attached to the ceiling. He held a gleaming knife over his head, as if poised to stab the chicken.

"*Ro op ringy pora ringo thingo stinko,*" he chanted. "*Hoo! Hoo! Hoo! Rubby! Reno beeno poker keeno! Debobo!*"

He was so into this weird ceremony that he didn't even see me standing in the doorway. "Hello?" I called.

He looked up sharply, scowling at me. He growled in annoyance. "Now I gotta start my voodoo ritual all over again!" he snarled.

I took two more steps farther into the shack. "Voodoo ritual?" I questioned.

"I'm about to sacrifice this chicken," he said,

swatting at the hanging chicken and sending it swinging.

I felt the need to point out the obvious. "Your chicken is not alive."

"You figured that out when you saw it ain't got a head," he said slyly. "Very smart."

I didn't know what to say. Was he goofing on me or was he serious? "Well, I —"

"I got some evil voodoo rituals to do!" he shouted. "And there ain't no live chickens on this island! You gonna volunteer to find me a live chicken?"

This guy was truly weird. And now he was screaming at me. "No, but —"

"Then shut up!"

How rude! I wasn't going to be bullied by some freaky Voodoo Maestro. I had a case to solve!

"Listen," I said. "I'm looking for clues regarding the reported demonic possession of college students."

"Here's a clue — purple and green are fall colors. It's the middle of May!" he yelled.

I stared at him, stunned. He was pointing at my dress. Was he questioning my fashion sense? "What?" I asked at last.

The Voodoo Maestro stood. He was tall and looked even taller with the dark shadows surrounding him. "Get off this island," he warned, stepping toward me.

I forced myself not to run. He took another step closer to me, but I stayed where I was.

"Get away from here before evil befalls your skinny, aerobicized butt!" he shouted. "And whatever you do, don't go into the Spooky Island castle."

He pointed out the shack's window. I looked and saw a big castle that looked like it once belonged to Count Dracula. The full moon had risen and it lit the castle in shimmering, eerie light. I wondered what a castle was doing on this creepy tropical island. I supposed it might be one of the attractions.

I wasn't falling for that old "don't go up to the castle" trick, though. I knew better than *that*! I was onto him.

"Aha!" I cried knowingly. "You *want* me to go up to the castle!"

"I just said *don't* go there!" he cried, sounding frustrated.

I was confused.

"But you're scary and you knew I'd do the opposite of what you said," I said. "So you figured

I'd go up to the castle, where you've set a trap to capture me! Very clever, but not clever enough!"

He shook his head, looking puzzled.

It made me wonder. Had I figured this out correctly? "Unless you knew I'd figure you out," I said, rethinking things. "So you told me not to go to the castle, so I'd think that you wanted me to go to the castle, so I wouldn't go . . . just how you didn't want me to . . ."

I had it! I'd figured it out!

"Ha!" I cried. "Well, I wasn't born yesterday in a barn, Mr. Creepy Voodoo Man! I'll find what you're hiding in that castle."

The Voodoo Maestro just stared at me. He seemed a little confused.

But I wasn't confused. Not anymore. I knew exactly what I had to do. Nothing was going to keep me out of that castle now. Not anything!

SHAGGY

Dead Mike's Bar and Grill was exactly what you'd expect the tavern at the Spooky Island Hotel to be like. There were pictures of monsters, ghosts, and zombies hanging all over the place. Fake spiderwebs hung in every doorway.

But in some ways, it was like any other nightspot. There were tables around the room. It had a disco ball and a few video game machines. In fact, it had the greatest, the granddaddy of all video games — Pong!

"Like, can you believe it — Pong!" I cried as Scooby, Mary Jane, and I walked into the place.

"Pong!" Mary Jane cried. "The king of all video games!" This woman had everything — beauty, style, Scooby Snacks, and a deep love of Pong.

"Let's play," I suggested.

"Definitely!" she agreed. "But first I have to find Bethanne."

She gazed around the place. "Bethanne's got to be here somewhere," she murmured.

A phone rang from behind the bar and the bartender picked it up. "I have a call for a Mr. Doo," he announced. "We got a Mr. Doo here?"

A college-type dude sat at the bar. He lifted himself off his seat. "I'm Melvin Doo," he said.

The bartender checked with the caller. "No. The call is for a Scooby-Doo."

Scooby grabbed the phone. "Rello?"

He listened for a minute, then nodded, and licked his lips. He put the phone back and then raced out the door.

"He looked awfully eager to go somewhere," Mary Jane observed.

"Like, I know," I replied. I stepped closer to the bartender. "Do you know what that was about?" I asked him.

"The guy on the other end said it was important. He said he had some hamburgers for Mr. Doo."

I scratched my head, thinking. *Who the heck would be giving Scooby hamburgers?*

VELMA

Nothing was going to stop me from solving this case. I wouldn't give up searching for clues, even if it meant I didn't sleep at all that night.

I followed the shoreline, making my way by the light of the full moon. Suddenly, I stopped. I'd come to a very large stone platform. A large stone bowl sat in the middle of the platform. All around the platform stood the same kind of demonic statues we'd seen earlier.

Behind the platform was a giant demonic head. It was striped and had large, bulging eyes. Two sharp horns jutted out of its head. Its open mouth was the size of a doorway.

Stepping onto the platform, I walked up to the big, shallow bowl. Moonlight danced inside it, revealing etchings of demons carved into the floor.

"Hey!" a voice bellowed.

I jumped, my heart thumping. I whirled around and faced a live skeleton.

Then I realized he was only a man painted to look like a skeleton. I assumed he was one of Mondavarious's strangely attired workers. Had he come out of the opening in the monster face's mouth?

"Jinkies, you scared me," I greeted him. "I was just looking at this attraction. Listen, may I ask you something? Have you noticed anything unusual since you've worked here — any visitors exhibiting unusual feats of strength?"

He shook his head. Just then I sensed movement from behind the statues. Two men stepped out of the shadows and came toward us.

Both of them were very large. One appeared to be Mexican and was dressed like a wrestler. A mask covered the upper half of his face.

The other was a very tall man who wore a tattered orange velvet jacket with tattered pants. His bald head was covered in tattoos.

He spoke first, but didn't seem to be talking to me. "Welcome, dear victims," he said in a bizarre accent I couldn't identify. I looked behind and saw that a crowd of college kids was assembling around the platform.

"My name is N'goo Tauna!" he continued.

"And this is my evil best pal, Zarkos! You may recognize him from Univision as the famous masked wrestler — Zarkos!"

A man in an island native outfit banged a gong. I jumped! I hadn't even noticed him or the gong before.

The moment the gong sounded, a lick of flame shot up from the center of the bowl. It must have gone up seven feet!

Men in grass skirts, wild headdresses, and face paint suddenly appeared around the platform. They began doing some kind of a frenzied war dance. It seemed I'd stumbled into a full-scale weirdo musical production number.

I peered out at the audience. In the light of the fire, I saw their faces. They were college kids, but there was something very strange about them. They didn't talk to one another, and they wore blank expressions.

I didn't like this whole thing. It was frightening me.

N'goo circled the flaming bowl. He spoke in a loud, scary voice. "This evil island is a thoroughfare to the demon realm," he cried. "For centuries it was home to cannibals who ate only the left arm of their victims, and buried the rest . . . alive!"

Ew, yuck, I thought, wishing I were up at the hotel hanging out with the rest of the gang.

"Then missionaries came and ended the practice by sewing the cannibals mouths shut and then burying them — alive!" N'goo shouted louder and louder. He was whipping himself into a state of wild excitement.

"Then the U.S. government tested nuclear weapons here, creating a bizarre series of mutations," he continued. "And then in 1991, during the first and only concert by Cher and Vanilla Ice, two college students found themselves possessed by demonic influences. Nine months later, the Olsen twins were born!"

"I think he's making this up as he goes along," I muttered to the guy beside me.

"But none of that matters, because ten years ago, a reckless businessman, Emile Mondavarious, *mocked* this sacred ground by building a theme park here."

N'goo stepped closer to the flame. His face seemed lit with demonic fire. "The demons are furious, my friends!" his voice boomed. "I assure you, while you party, they plot their revenge."

He swung his hands around the fire in wild gestures. As he did, the flame burst up even higher, exploding into fireworks. Horrible-looking demons flew out of the colorful, sparkling lights.

The zombielike crowd gasped and stepped back in fright. One of them dropped to his knees in terror. He stared, goggle-eyed, at the demons zooming around the fire.

My eyes darted around the scene, trying to take it all in — to understand what was going on. And then I saw something that made everything very clear.

N'goo chuckled triumphantly. He shifted his gaze to me. "Do my friends frighten you?" he taunted.

"They would," I admitted. "If it weren't for those projectors." I nodded toward the bases of the statues, where small lenses projected the demonic images into the air. "There. There. And there," I pointed them out, as if he didn't already know.

N'goo laughed bitterly. "What a smart young woman you are." He ruffled my hair as if I were a dog! I slapped his hand away, and the crowd laughed as though it were the funniest thing they'd ever seen.

SCOOBY

Rin ra rorest ri raw a rign rat raid RAMRURGERS RHIS RAY. Rit ras rary, rut ri ras rungry. Rand ri rove RAMRURGERS. Ri rollowed ra rigns runtil ri round a rag.

Re rag ras rempty! Ro RAMRURGERS! Ri ras ricked!

Ren a ronster rame! Rikes! Ri ran!

Rit rhased re. Ri ran rand ran rack ro Read Rike's!

(A note from Shaggy:

What Scoob was trying to say here was that he went into the forest and followed signs that said HAMBURGERS THIS WAY. He followed all the signs. He was scared, but he loves HAMBURG-ERS so much. He kept following signs until he came to the bag of yummy hamburgers. But the bag was empty. There were no HAMBURGERS! He had been been tricked. Then, a horrible, awful, hideous monster came. Scooby ran away, all the way back to Dead Mike's.)

SHAGGY

The Pong ball blipped across the screen in Dead Mike's Bar and Grill. I was in heaven. Mary Jane and I were playing our 567th game. I didn't even know who was winning. I didn't care. I was playing Pong with, like, the love of my life, and that was all that mattered.

"I can't believe it," I said to her. "We both play the bongos. We both know how to shuffle cold cuts. You and me, we're, like, the same guy, except you're not a guy."

"I know," Mary Jane said with an adorable giggle. "It's, like, zoinks!"

Zoinks? Did she say *zoinks*? She had! Amazing!

I wanted to do something great for Mary Jane, something that showed her how much I cared. A stuffed animal crane machine stood just a few feet away. "Hey! Want a stuffed thing?" I asked.

Mary Jane smiled but shook her head. "Nobody can win at those things."

I grinned at her. She still had a lot to learn about me. I pumped the machine with two quarters and began working the controls. "Fred says it's a useless talent," I told her as I worked. "He says I should have, like, learned French instead. But I'm the ace of the crane machine."

"I think being good at a crane machine is way, way better than French," Mary Jane said. She put her hand on my shoulder and watched me grab a dismembered green monster head and crank it up. Her touch almost made me drop the stuffed head, but I forced myself to be cool as I carefully placed the head in the bin.

I handed it to her. "I'm glad I couldn't find Bethanne," she said, smiling at her furry stuffed head. "It's been nice spending time with you."

Those were the sweetest words I'd ever heard. We were standing close, almost nose to nose. "Mary Jane," I said.

"Shaggy," she whispered back.

This was it. The moment was right. I was about to kiss the girl I'd been waiting for all my life.

Then — *blam*! The next thing I knew, Scooby had leaped into my arms.

"Raggy! A ronster!"

"Scooby!" I yelled, dropping him. I could see he was, like, terrified. He was panting hard and his eyes were popping with fright. Then, a goofy-looking monster that was *obviously* a man in a mask ran into Dead Mike's. *This* was what Scooby was afraid of? "Like, quit goofing around, Scoob!"

Scooby looked embarrassed.

Mary Jane let out a burst of sneezes. "I better go see if Bethanne's at the hotel," she said. "It's okay if you don't want to, but if you wanted we could maybe meet up later on?"

"Groovy," I told her.

Mary Jane smiled at me and waved to Scoob. "Bye, Scooby." She held the stuffed head up to my cheek and pretended it was kissing me. It wasn't the kiss I wanted, but it would have to do for now.

I watched her walk out, then turned to Scooby. "What's going on?" I asked. "I was just about to —"

I didn't finish because Daphne walked in and called to us. "Shaggy! Scooby!" She seemed excited.

FRED

 After Daphne ran off — chasing that weird guy she was following from the boardwalk — I found some clues on my own.

Really big footprints! "Score," I whispered.

They led from the boardwalk into the woods. I followed them by moonlight all the way up to a creepy-looking castle.

I passed signs that said, DANGER! DO NOT ENTER, and BEWARE! I didn't pay attention to them, though. I was on a case. These big footprints kept going past the signs and I was going to follow them, no matter what.

When I finally came out past the trees, I gazed up at the frightening castle. Up close, I could see that it had once been a ride. Now it appeared to be shut down. In front of it stood three of those bizarre demon statues.

"Fred!" someone shouted, sounding very angry. I didn't have to look to know who it was, but I turned slowly.

Daphne stomped her foot. Scooby and Shaggy were with her. "Go away!" she cried. "I found this place! I call dibs on its clues!"

She wasn't getting away with that. No way! "I already found clues," I insisted.

"What?" she challenged, not believing me.

I pointed to one of the big footprints. "I followed these weird footprints. Whatever made them could be dangerous."

"We'll go away," Shaggy volunteered. "Scoob and I don't do castles."

"No! You two stay right there," Daphne ordered. Then she faced me angrily. "Look, Fred, I don't need you to save me. If anyone messes with me, I'll open a can of two-thousand-year-old martial arts on 'em."

In a flash, one of the statues reached out and grabbed Daphne from behind. Daphne shrieked.

I was ready to jump on the statue, but then I heard laughter — familiar laughter. The statue loosened its grip and Velma came out from behind it, giggling.

"What are you doing here?" I asked her.

"This castle ride was closed due to dangerous

construction," she replied. "It's the most likely place to hatch an evil plan. Besides, I wanted to scare the heck out of Daphne."

Daphne glared at the two of us.

I hadn't planned on everyone meeting up here. But since we were all together, I figured it was up to me to come up with a plan — like I always did.

"Okay, gang," I said. "Let's split up and look for more clues. Daphne, you and I —"

"Typical!" Velma interrupted angrily.

"What?" I asked.

"I was always picked last for the teams," she said. "Your little groups. You and Daphne over here, Shaggy and Scooby over there."

"Fine," I said. "Daphne, you enter through the entrance. Velma and I will enter here, through the exit. And Shaggy and Scooby, do whatever you guys do."

Shaggy and Scooby went over to a door marked STAFF ONLY.

"Scoobert, open the door," Shaggy instructed.

"Rhy re?" Scooby asked.

"Because if a monster tears your head off you, I'll have a warning," Shaggy explained.

Scooby shot him a look, but opened the door.

Velma and I went in the exit door. Inside it

was cold and dim. Life-size models of knights held crossbows that were aimed right at us. Animatronic robotic monks, executioners, and a jester stood there. They looked awfully lifelike. And they were like those pictures you see in museums sometimes—the eyes seemed to follow you everywhere.

"Jinkies," Velma whispered.

Hearing her say that brought back a lot of memories. I suddenly felt a wave of tenderness for good old Velma. "Velma," I said, "I never meant to, you know, pick you last."

"Don't worry about it," she said gruffly. "I know you, Fred. All you care about are thin, good-looking babes."

I couldn't believe that she thought I was that shallow. She had me all wrong! "No," I insisted. "I'm a man of substance. Dorky chicks like you turn me on every now and again."

She shot me a dirty look.

"What?" I asked. "That's a compliment."

At that moment, there was a loud bang. It sounded like a big lever being pulled.

From all around the room, eerie eyes glowed, staring at us. The animatronic figures had come to life! They lifted their heads and began to move.

SHAGGY

 "Like, yikes, Scooby!" I shouted as the castle came to life. Suddenly the dark, quiet place was, like, loud! Gears, pulleys, and winches all creaked and banged as the row of rusty cars that had once been part of the ride came to life.

A robot jester jerked his head back and began cackling in a seriously creepy way. His eyes glowed with a horrible green light.

"I've got a bad feeling about this, Scoob," I said.

From the terrified, wide-eyed look on his face, I guessed he did, too.

Scooby and I ran into the next room. It was like some kind of banquet hall with a long table in the middle. Rows of sausages, poultry, and hams hung from the walls. "This is better," I said to Scoob.

He nodded and tried to eat one of the

sausages. He made a disgusted face. "Rastic," he reported.

"Plastic?" I said. "Bummer." I joined Scooby to look at the plastic sausages when, suddenly, the sausage links sprang at us! They coiled around Scooby and me, strapping us tightly against the wall.

"I have a really, *really* bad feeling about this," I said to Scooby.

"Relp!" Scooby yelled.

"Help!" I joined him. We kept it up for a few minutes, but no one came.

"We'll have to do what we do best, Scoob," I suggested. "Eat!"

"Rit's rastic!" Scooby protested.

"I know it's plastic," I said. "But, dude, you drink out of the toilet. A little plastic isn't going to hurt you."

What else could we do? We started chomping on the plastic sausage.

It wasn't easy. We kept chewing and chewing. "Reminds me of the time we tried to eat the guy in the hot dog costume," I said between bites.

Scooby just burped. I laughed and he burped again.

My stomach made a rude noise. "I don't feel so good," I said.

VELMA

Everything was happening so fast! When the robots came to life, Fred and I raced into another room. Two of the walls were covered in bookshelves. A large mirror covered the far wall of the room. I finally felt safe. *Bang!* The door slammed shut behind us.

We were trapped.

And just when things couldn't get any worse, a giant, sparkling blade descended from the ceiling. It began swinging wildly back and forth across the room. A mechanical jester rode it, laughing evilly. We had to jump out of its path to keep from becoming sliced meat.

We bumped up against the bookshelves. The books all appeared to be ancient volumes. I knew one of them had to open a secret passageway. "Help me, Fred," I urged him. I began flinging books off the shelves. "If we can open to a passage it might be our only way out."

The blade continued swinging. Fortunately, we were crouched far enough out of its path to be safe. My hair flew around my face, blown by a wind the blade created. We knocked every single book off that shelf — but we still hadn't opened a secret passage.

"Maybe I can open that door," Fred considered.

"But what about the blade?" It was now swinging so widely that it went from the mirrored wall and back to the door on the other side. It was moving fast, too.

"What choice do we have?" He waited till the blade moved away from the door, then leaped in front of it and began jiggling the door handle, trying to force the door open.

I kept my eyes on the blade. My heart pounded. Fred was taking too much time! In seconds, the sharp point would plunge right into Fred's back.

"Fred!" I shouted a warning.

He kept working on the door, ignoring me.

Fred!" I screamed. He turned, just as the blade was about to hit him.

I did the only thing I could think of. I scooped up a thick book and tossed it to him to use as a shield.

He caught it and held it up to his chest. At that moment, the blade sank into the book, cutting straight through it. The blade tossed Fred and the book high into the air and Fred went crashing through the mirrored wall.

There was a horrible grinding sound, and the blade came to a sudden stop. I ran to the broken mirror and peered through. There was a room on the other side. About twenty metal folding chairs were set up in rows in the middle. It looked like a small theater or a conference room.

Right below me was some sort of control panel, and Fred had landed right on top of it. His crash landing had probably turned off the blade. "Nice teamwork, Fred," I complimented him.

He looked up at me, grinning. "Good plan, Velma."

I glanced to my side and saw that we'd forgotten to toss one single book off the shelf. Just to see, I tossed it to the floor. A door swung open, and I was able to walk right into the conference room. It figured.

Fred and I explored the room. "Looks like some sort of school," he said.

"Yeah," I agreed. "P.S. one-twenty-weird." I leaned my hand down on a VCR that stood on a side table. I must have pushed a button, because an image suddenly appeared on the viewing screen in front of us.

At first I thought it was *MTV Spring Break*. A bunch of college kids in bathing suits were having a wild party on the beach. They didn't look very different from the kids who had come to Spooky Island with us. An announcer — a pretty young woman — stood in front of them, speaking to the audience.

"Welcome to America," she said in a peppy, clear announcer's voice. "I am using the language English. Now that you're a young adult, you will need to learn societal do's and don'ts."

Fred and I exchanged a bewildered glance. What was this all about?

DAPHNE

 Coming to this castle was my big idea. I admit it. I was definitely regretting it, though.

First, the entire castle jumped into an animatronic, robotic frenzy. Then the cars of the old ride barreled toward me, scooped me up, and took me for a hairdo-destroying ride around the entire castle.

As I was being carried along on the front car, I saw this small man scurrying by. He could have been the eighth dwarf — Creepy. I called out to him for help, but he just chuckled and ran off in another direction.

All of a sudden, the cart stopped, and so did everything else. It was as if someone had hit the OFF switch.

I climbed out and came to a round room. There was a podium in the middle, and on top of that stood a little pyramid, about the size of a flowerpot. The moment I picked it up, a cage began falling from the ceiling.

Thanks to my keen instincts, honed by martial arts training, I was able to leap out of the way. I avoided being captured yet again. I was definitely succeeding at that, at least.

With the pyramid in my hand, I ran through the castle. A weird sound and awful smell came from a room, so I stopped to investigate. I found Scooby and Shaggy having a burp and fart contest in a room filled with gnawed plastic meat. Disgusting!

"We're here. To solve. A mystery," I told them.

But they couldn't seem to stop laughing. So I left them there and returned to the round room to examine the pyramid. I gazed over at the cage that now covered the podium. This pyramid was very important to someone.

I noticed some writing etched at the bottom of the pyramid. In the shadowy light it was hard to see, but I made out the words *Daemon Ritus*. What on earth was that?

FRED

Velma and I continued watching the strange show playing on the TV screen. We weren't exactly sure what we were watching, but it was bizarre.

We saw two actors acting out a skit. They were college guys, just like in the other scenes. One guy carried a box, the other drank a soda. They passed each other and accidentally bumped shoulders.

"Sorry, bro," the guy with the box apologized.

The guy with the soda went ballistic, though. "I will crush your bones into dust!" he threatened.

The scene paused, and the perky announcer returned. "Let's see how the situation *should* be handled," she said.

The actors began the scene again. "Sorry, bro," the guy with the box repeated.

"No big whoop, dog. Yo, you check out that new video on the box?" replied the guy with the soda. His hostile attitude was gone.

"Word," the box guy replied as the scene faded out.

The announcer returned. "Interaction between adults is more formal."

A new scene appeared on the screen. A young man walked into an office. Inside the office, a guy in a suit sat behind a desk. The young man sat in the chair opposite him. They looked at each other across the desk.

"So, you're here to apply for a job," the businessman began.

"Yes, sir," the young man replied.

"Can you share with me some of your specific skills?" suit guy requested.

"Here's one," the young man answered. He stood up and — with superhuman strength — lifted the desk into the air. Then he began beating the guy in the suit with it.

This scene froze and the announcer returned. "Let's see how the situation *should* be handled." The actors ran through the scene again. Only, this time, the young man told suit guy his skills and the two shook hands at the end.

This was all just too weird for me. I didn't

know what to make of it. "What do you think?" I asked Velma, who sat beside me.

"It seems to be a brainwashing facility of some sort," she said.

That made sense. "Perhaps this is the home base of some cult," I offered. "Maybe they steal the minds of young people who come to Spooky Island."

Velma nodded. "And wherever there's a brainwashing cult there has to be a power-hungry leader behind it all. The Papa Smurf figure."

"Mondavarious?" I suggested.

Velma considered for a moment. "No," she said. "If he was the one, why would he have called us here?"

That was true. We still hadn't found out who was behind all this. But at least this case was beginning to unfold. "Let's hope our teammates are finding equally intriguing clues," I said.

An alarm siren suddenly screamed through the halls of the castle. What was going on?

Velma and I jumped up from our chairs and raced out into a hallway lined with suits of armor. Daphne, Shaggy, and Scooby ran down the hall toward us. I noticed that Daphne clutched a small pyramid in her hands.

Together, we all ran toward a door at the far end of the long hallway.

"Sounds like they're on to us!" I shouted. "We'd better get out of here."

"I found neat and scary clues," Daphne told us as we continued running.

"Us, too!" Velma said. "We think this is a brainwashing facility for an evil cult."

Daphne held up her pyramid. "Maybe this is the sacred relic-thingie that they worship."

We were nearly to the door but we all stopped short. The doorknob was turning. Someone — or something — was on the other side and was about to come in.

We were trapped!

Or maybe not.

"Quick, gang," I said in a hurried whisper. "Pretend you're part of the display."

We all raced around, grabbing costumes off animatronic robots, striking poses, pretending we belonged there. Shaggy and I clanged together as we struggled into knight's armor. Daphne pulled a princess's dress and crown off a robot, kicked the robot into the corner, and pulled on the outfit. Velma did the same with wizard's robes. Scooby found fake fangs somewhere, put them in his mouth, and struck a dragon's pose.

The door flew open and we froze. A very strange-looking wrestling guy in a mask marched in, flanked by some guys in native dress.

Velma gasped quietly. "Zarkos!" she murmured.

They moved down the hallway, glancing from side to side. One of the native guys carried a torch, which he used to light their way.

A small, creepy-looking guy ran down the hall to meet them. "Sir, they found the Daemon Ritus," the little guy told the one Velma called Zarkos.

"All right," Zarkos said angrily. "It's time to summon the big muchachos."

DAPHNE

That Daemon Ritus pyramid thing was closer than that wrestler creep could have imagined. I stood just feet away from him, holding it. I'd thrown a cloak over the hand that held it, but if I'd made even the slightest move he might have seen it.

I tried to be as silent as I could. I barely dared to breathe.

Finally, Zarkos and his men stomped off down the hall. The moment they were gone, we raced through the door onto some stairs that led out of the castle.

We pulled off our costumes and — without even discussing it — we all just began running toward the hotel.

We finally made it back, safe and sound. In the lobby we stopped, panting for breath. I felt strangely happy, and the rest of the gang seemed to feel that way, too. All of them seemed lit up with some kind of inner excitement.

Mr. Mondavarious came down the stairs. "You all seem rather cheery," he observed. "Good news, I hope."

"Mr. Mononucleosis —" Fred greeted him.

"Mondavarious! Do try to keep up," Mondavarious corrected him sharply.

Fred didn't seem to notice. "We've hit a clue smorgasbord," he continued. "We believe someone on the island is running a secret brainwashing operation."

Mondavarious covered his heart with his hand and stepped back in shock. "Brainwashing? No!"

"Back up," Shaggy said to Fred. "What's this about a smorgasbord?"

"A smorgasbord of clues, not food," I told him.

His face fell in disappointment. "When is this all-you-can-eat thing going to start?"

"Who could be behind such a thing?" Mondavarious wondered out loud, ignoring Shaggy's question.

"The masked wrestler is involved somehow," Velma informed him.

"Zarkos?" Mondavarious questioned skeptically. "He's not clever enough to be the ring-leader."

"All right, then," I spoke up. "We have three leading suspects as to who's behind this evil hoody."

"N'goo Tauna," Velma named the first suspect. "He believes your theme park's been built on sacred ground."

"The voodoo man, who shrewdly tricked me into going to the castle," I named the second.

"And *you*!" Fred said, pointing an accusing finger at Mondavarious.

Mondavarious gasped. "Me?"

Fred didn't seem to care that Mondavarious looked like he was about to faint. He turned to the rest of us, forgetting all about the shocked Mondavarious. "Okay, gang," he said. "Let's meet in a half hour. I'll interview employees to see if they've noticed anything odd."

"I'll get to work on translating these hiero-glyphics Daphne found," Velma said.

I wondered what I should do. Then I had an idea. "I'll research cults on the Net." Velma shot me a high five and I fived her back.

Mondavarious was still looking pale. "I'm a suspect?" he asked again.

Fred patted his shoulder. "Don't take it personally. It's mostly just because you creep me out."

Mondavarious appeared to be relieved by this. "Oh, I see," he said, color coming back to his cheeks. "Thank you."

Just then, Shaggy's girlfriend from the plane came into the lobby. "Hey!" Shaggy greeted her dreamily. He walked over to her and smiled.

"Why are you acting so loopy?" his new girlfriend asked.

"What just happened brings a groovy tear to my heart. The gang's back together," Shaggy told her.

"That's great," she said. "But I'm starting to worry about my friend Bethanne. I can't find her anywhere."

I began to worry, too. What if something had happened to her friend?

VELMA

I set up a study in Dead Mike's Bar and Grill. Actually, it was just a table with the Daemon Ritus sitting on it. I was examining the scary drawings on the pyramid.

The drawings were way creepy — a monstrous figure pulling a bubble out of a human, a bubble with an arrow pointing to a human, a monster crawling into a human's mouth.

What could they mean? And why was this pyramid so important? Did it do anything? Was it a symbol of something? I was sure that once I figured it out, the mystery would begin to unravel.

Looking up, I noticed a guy I'd met on the plane coming toward me. I didn't know his name, but I thought of him as Metal Head, since he looked like someone who was into heavy-metal rock.

He stopped by my table. "Hey! Did your friends ditch you?"

"No," I said, laughing. "I always do the book work."

"Can I buy you a drink? A Bloody Skull?" he offered.

I don't drink, but I'd already had a Bloody Skull. I knew it was made of tomato juice and celery juice. That was all.

"Okeydoke," I agreed.

Metal Head ordered the drinks, then sat down beside me. "What's that dealie?" he asked, pointing to the Daemon Ritus pyramid.

"It's called the Daemon Ritus, but I don't really know why," I explained. "The text reminds me of Babylonian hieroglyphics. I can make out some of it. It looks like instructions for some type of sacred ritual. It's fascinating!"

The bartender came over with two skull mugs and put one in front of each of us.

"You really dig doing this, huh?" Metal Head said. On the plane, I'd told him a little about how the gang and I solved mysteries. He'd sort of remembered reading about us. "You dig all these clues and stuff?" he asked.

"Certainly," I said. "Really focusing on a mystery reminds me of the old days."

For a moment, I forgot all about Metal Head and drifted off into a memory of when the gang and I were so tight and worked as a team. It came back to me so clearly.

"It used to be great," I said out loud to Metal Head — but really more to myself. "Daphne was so rich and beautiful, but she never pretended to be better than anyone else. And we all looked up to Fred — he was the most popular kid at Coolsville High."

I laughed, thinking about all the funny things Scooby and Shaggy had done. "Shaggy and Scooby were such cards, always getting into trouble and making us laugh," I told Metal Head. "Those were the best times. I had friends I really liked and they loved the same thing I loved best of all — solving mysteries."

"Wow!" Metal Head said. "It sounds perfect."

"Well, almost," I said, sighing. "We did have one big problem — a little dog with a huge ego, Scrappy-Doo. He was very overexcited, to put it mildly. He was always yelling, 'Scrappy-Dappy-Doo!' and threatening to pulverize the bad guys with puppy power."

What a pest that little dog had been. He never really fit in with the rest of us. We all found him annoying. We used to take him with us on cases because he was Scooby's nephew. But he annoyed us to death. Then one afternoon, he announced that the time had come for us to appoint him as our unquestioned leader. None of us could believe it. But that was the last straw. We left him standing on the side of the road and took off.

Metal Head walked to the bar and ordered us another two drinks. "Puppy power, huh?" he said as he sat back down.

"He wasn't even a puppy," I said. "That was a gland disorder."

The bartender brought over two more Bloody Skulls. I was starting to feel a little giddy. That N'goo guy was playing piano and it sounded lovely.

I noticed Shaggy and Mary Jane come in and sit together. Scooby came in alone and sat by himself. He looked sad, like he'd lost his best friend.

A few minutes later, Daphne and Fred walked in. They didn't seem to be angry with each other anymore. They sat at a table together. It made me happy to be around all my old pals again.

But then, Scooby jumped up and let out a terrible scream! Everyone in the place turned to stare at him. He pointed toward the window.

"Ronsters!" he shouted.

Just then, it happened. The lights went out, and the whole hotel was shrouded in darkness. Everyone in Dead Mike's looked around nervously.

"It's probably just an electrical failure. Like everything else, it has a simple scientific explanation," Fred said.

"Ronsters!" Scooby shrieked again.

Fred looked embarrassed. "Scooby, how many times do I have to tell you? There are no such entities as ghosts, ghouls, goblins, or monsters! At the end of every paranormal claim there are only fools seeking fame, paranoid imaginations, or charlatans looking to make a buck! There are absolutely — absolutely — no such things as —"

But before Fred could finish, a twelve-foot horned demon smashed his way through the window, sending glass flying in all directions. His flattened head was sunk into his monstrously muscular body. His horrible claws must have been three feet long! His body was transparent, like a ghost. It was safe to say that this was no man in a mask!

SHAGGY

The demon grabbed Fred by the back of his shirt and lifted him high into the air. I wanted to help but, like, I didn't know how.

"Save Daphne!" Fred yelled bravely. Before he could say anything else, the demon breathed on him. Out came a green mist that knocked Fred out cold. Talk about your bad breath!

All the college kids in the place were going berserk-o. They, like, ran screaming for the doorways.

One of them knocked off Velma's glasses. She's totally blind without them. She began groping around the table, searching for them.

At least Daphne was thinking. She saw the demon heading toward the Daemon Ritus, sitting on Velma's table. With lightning speed she dashed past it and tossed the pyramid into her purse.

Then another demon came crashing down through the ceiling skylight. He landed easily in a crouch on the floor. He opened his jaws and let out a piercing, mind-blowing shriek.

I grabbed Mary Jane by the wrist and pulled her behind the bar with me — just in time, too! The demon passed right over us, not looking down. "This is, like, the opposite of what I wanted to do today," I said to Mary Jane as I tried to keep my teeth from chattering.

I peeked over the side of the bar to see how my pals were doing. The first one I saw was Velma, and my jaw dropped. Someone had found her glasses and was handing them to her.

That someone was a demon!

She put on her glasses and looked up at him. I expected her to scream. But she didn't. "Nice mask," I heard her say.

The demon lifted her into the air — but she still seemed to think he was only a guy in a mask. She yanked at his horns as if she expected the mask to come flying off. She managed to stretch the horns, but they only snapped back into place. "Jinkies!" she cried. The demon breathed his green mist on her, and she conked out, too, just like Fred.

The second demon chased Mondavarious, who had come in to see what was going on. Daphne leaped in between them and struck a karate pose. "Back, sir," she ordered Mondavarious. "I will protect you!"

"Yikes!" I screamed as a demon hand smashed up through the floorboards next to Daphne. But it didn't grab her — it grabbed Mondavarious and pulled him through the floor. Then another hand appeared and grabbed at her, but she slapped at it and yanked her leg away. She ran into the stairwell — but the demons cornered her there. She was trapped while big, scary demons leered at her. But wait — was that *Scooby* with them? It was! He was trying to pretend he was a demon — as cover! But, like, the demons figured that out at the exact same time I did. And they came after him!

Well, at least Daphne got to escape. The demons chased Scooby down the hall.

"What's happening out there?" Mary Jane asked me.

Peeking back over the bar I saw that the room was now full of demons. There were more than twenty of them. One of them spotted me and let out a high-pitched wail. All the demons turned in our direction. Their eyes glowed green and they all began screaming.

I jumped onto the bar and pulled Mary Jane up with me. "Come on, Daphne," I called as Mary Jane and I scrambled over the bar. "It's time to start running!"

But where was Scooby? "Scooby-Doo, where are you?" I hollered.

DAPHNE

Thank god for giant vases. Scooby, Shaggy, Mary Jane, and I each dove into a vase that stood in front of the hotel and managed to hide until the demons left. Of course, that was only after they'd chased us up, over, under, and around every inch of the hotel.

Once it had been quiet for a good long time, we popped our heads out of the vase openings, one at a time. Shaggy and I were the first ones up. "I have the sinking feeling these dudes aren't brainwashed cult members," Shaggy said to me.

I sighed and nodded. That much was clear enough. "Then what are they?" I asked. "And what do they want with these students? And why had that man with the tattooed head tried to get the Daemon Ritus? We need to follow them."

Shaggy looked at me like I was deranged. "We need to what?"

It seemed obvious enough to me. "So we can defeat the demons and save Fred and Velma," I explained.

Shaggy chuckled. "Oh, yeah. That's sort of like my plan — which is to get the heck out of here!"

"No way!" I cried. Fred and Velma always figured out everything. Now it was my turn! For the first time, they were the damsels in distress, not me.

I climbed out of the vase. The terrible smell of burning sulfur hung in the air. I figured it must have come from the demons. Shaggy, Mary Jane, and Scooby got out of their vases and I waved for them to follow me.

I hoped that if I followed the smell I could sniff out the demons' trail. It drew me down along the shoreline. I came to a large, round platform. Behind it stood a hideous demon face with sharp horns and bulging eyes. Its wide mouth looked like a gruesome doorway.

The demons appeared, crashing through the palm trees and underbrush. They carried unconscious students. I recognized one of them as the guy Velma had been sitting with. I'd seen the other ones in the bar, also.

We ducked behind some nearby palm trees.

Scooby jumped into Shaggy's arms and began shivering with fear. "I know how you feel, Scoob," Shaggy said. "I don't like the looks of this, either."

Mary Jane took a cell phone from her back pocket and began dialing. She saw me staring at her. "I'm dialing for help," she explained.

"No. I've got this," I explained. "I've got this."

I turned away from her and back to spy on the demons.

But they were gone — totally and completely vanished. It was as if the scary platform had swallowed them up. "I don't get this," I murmured. In fact, I hadn't the slightest idea of what to do next.

"We'll keep watch," I declared, trying to sound more confident than I felt. Shaggy, Scooby, and Mary Jane looked nervous, but they agreed.

The next thing I knew, something hard banged against my head. A line of throbbing pain ran across my head like a band. I bolted straight up and found a volleyball in my lap.

A volleyball had hit me on the head!

The sun burned in my eyes. Rock 'n' roll blared from a radio behind me. Scooby, Shaggy, and Mary Jane still slept. But the beach was full of college kids. Some swam, some laughed and

chased each other. Others sunned themselves —
and still others played volleyball.

I guess we must have fallen asleep while we
were keeping watch. It was as if last night had
never happened. Had it been a dream?

No. Definitely not. If it had been, then why
would we be sleeping here on the beach? "Something messed up is happening," I said to myself.

"Yo! Red! The ball," called a young woman I
remembered from the other day. She had been a
snooty, rich-girl type. (Like I might have been if I
hadn't discovered the world of detective work.)

But this girl was not the type to say *yo*. Her
entire personality was different than it had been
yesterday. And so was her bathing suit. Now she
was wearing a skimpy bikini. Yesterday I'd seen
her in a very unrevealing blue tank suit. She'd
made a drastic change overnight.

I tossed her the ball and got to my feet.
Shaggy, Mary Jane, and Scooby were rubbing
their eyes as they began to awaken. Shaggy
stretched and yawned. "I'm starved," he said
groggily.

"Come on," I said. "You can eat up at the hotel. I want to see what's going on up there."

I headed up the hill to the hotel and the others followed. What was going on up at the hotel was something like an episode of *MTV's Spring Break*. College kids jumped into the pool, spraying one another with bottles of soda. The girls wore little bikinis, the guys high-fived one another every chance they got. A lot of them danced to the music of a cool-sounding band that played at one end of the pool.

"Wow!" Mary Jane said. "It's Sugar Ray."

"Who's he?" I asked.

"Not he, them," she said, pointing to the band. "They're, like, my favorite band. There's the lead singer, Mark McGrath."

What was a famous band doing here on Spooky Island? I had to check it out. I walked around the pool to get a closer look at them.

As I stood watching, the lead singer noticed me. He began singing right to me. It was a kick at first, but after a while I started to feel uneasy. There was a look in the guy's eyes that scared me. It was a dangerous, mean look. I walked away and joined Mary Jane, Scooby, and Shaggy.

Looking back at Sugar Ray, I realized what it was that bothered me. There was something odd about the way the entire band moved. For a bunch of cool rock stars, they were awfully stiff.

With Velma and Fred gone, it was up to me to take the lead in this investigation. *What would*

Fred do right now? I wondered. I knew! He'd come up with a plan. "Let's split up and look for . . ." I couldn't remember how the rest of it went.

"Clues," Shaggy suggested.

"Right!" I said. That was it! "Try to find Fred and Velma."

"I'll go this way," Mary Jane said, pointing toward the hotel.

"Okay," I agreed.

I suddenly had the feeling someone was staring at me. Looking over at the band, I saw that it was Mark McGrath. I didn't like the eerie smile he shot my way. It sent a chill up my back.

"I'll go to the back of the hotel," I said, eager to get away from him.

As I hurried away I realized I hadn't given Shaggy and Scooby an assignment. Oh, well, they'd come up with something on their own. Although — what they usually came up with was trouble.

SHAGGY

"Hey, pal, look at this," I said as I knelt beside a deck chair. Bending low, I pulled a piece of red material from underneath it.

Scooby looked at me, confused.

"I think this is Fred's ascot," I explained. I leaned back on my heels. I couldn't even picture Fred without his ascot.

Scooby-Doo has a canine supersniffer that sure comes in handy on cases. I gave him a whiff of the material and he was instantly on the case.

He sniffed his way through the crowd of good-time college kids. He moved so fast it was hard to keep up with him.

Finally, he stopped short.

"*Red!*" he cried.

I looked at the dude standing in front of us. I was glad he smelled like Fred, because he sure

The Mystery, Inc. gang comes to life!
Meet Daphne, Fred, Scooby, Shaggy, and Velma.

Velma, Fred, and Shaggy arrive at Spooky Island, the site of the gang's latest case. They've been hired to investigate strange happenings at the tropical theme park.

But soon enough, Velma's face-to-face with creepy creatures . . .

... Shaggy gets captured by a sausage monster ...

... and Daphne discovers a strange pyramid with magical powers. Looks like there's a mystery to solve!

Jinkies! Velma examines the mysterious pyramid . . .

. . . while Daphne is serenaded by Mark McGrath of Sugar Ray. Little does she know that demons have stolen his soul!

Things get really weird when the gang's souls switch into different bodies! Now Fred is Daphne, Daphne is Velma, and Velma is Fred.

Back in their own bodies once more, Velma, Fred, and Shaggy go undercover to find out why the teenagers on Spooky Island are behaving so strangely.

Scooby-Doo, where are you? In the end, it's up to scaredy-cat Shaggy to face his fears and rescue his best bud.

And damsel-in-distress Daphne busts out and kicks some demon butt.

Once again, the gang bravely faces the bad guys
Another mystery solved!

didn't look like him. He wore sunglasses, a muscle–T, and shorts. No ascot.

He was with two other guys and didn't seem to see Shaggy and me. The other guys looked familiar to me. Then I realized who they were — Brad the Goth and the heavy-metal dude Velma had been sitting with. Only they were also way different than they'd looked yesterday.

Brad the Goth was now all cleaned up. He looked more like Brad the President of the Future Young Executives Club. His hair was neatly combed. He wore long board shorts. There wasn't a trace of leather or a metal stud anywhere.

And the heavy-metal guy was as cleaned up as Brad. In fact, the three of them looked alike, and they looked like all the other guys who were hanging around the pool.

"Yo! Yo! What she said was, like, *waaa* and I was, like, later on," Fred said to his friends in a voice that sounded as though he'd grown up in the valley instead of Coolsville, U.S.A. His new pals high-fived him and laughed.

Fred still didn't notice Scooby and me. I had to get his attention. "Fred! Fred!" I called.

He turned toward me, but his expression

didn't change. I wasn't sure if he even recognized us. What was going on with him? This was definitely not the Fred I knew.

Suddenly, Fred (or whoever he was) noticed us standing there. "What up, dog, and, uh . . . dog," he greeted us in that same not-Fred voice.

"Like, what happened last night?" I asked him.

"Man, we beats like was the lizz nizz on Earth. If you didn't get a fat Mack on, you needed to smack on, smack off, G. Know what I'm saying?"

"No," I answered. I had, like, no clue what he was saying. In fact, I felt totally clueless about everything altogether.

DAPHNE

The gang and I have solved a lot of cases, and I thought I'd seen just about everything. But I never, *ever* thought I'd see anything like this.

At the back of the hotel was an entry marked WOMEN ONLY. I decided to check it out. It led right into the ladies' locker room beside the indoor pool.

The scene inside was like a ladies-only version of the party at the outdoor pool. Young women in bikinis and towels boogied and strutted on the benches to music playing on a radio.

But that wasn't the shocking thing.

The shocking thing was Velma — without her glasses, wearing a bikini — and makeup!

She was shaking and dancing along with the rest of the strange crowd. I stood in front of her, but she didn't seem to recognize me. Maybe that was because she wasn't wearing her glasses, but something told me it was much worse than that.

"Velma!" I cried. "What the heck is going on?"

She wasn't in the least bit upset. She smiled at me and kept dancing.

"I'm getting my swerve on," she said. She shouted out to her new friends. "Am I right, ladies? Give it up now! All right! All right!"

One of the dancing beach babes shouted back, "You go, girl! You go!"

"What about those demons?" I insisted.

Velma strutted back and forth on the bench. "I got your demons right here. Yeah! Yeah! Do I hear it?"

She suddenly stopped midstrut. "Hold on," she said. "There is one thing about those demons I remember. The naff scream."

This was a good sign. She was remembering, coming around, back to her old self.

"Scream?" I asked.

"Uh-huh," Velma replied. She seemed to be remembering something. "It was sort of like . . ."

Velma's eyes slowly filled with red. Not allergy red, but bright, glowing red. I noticed the same thing happening to all the college girls around the room.

I began backing away, slowly.

I began freaking out, seriously!

Velma opened her mouth and let out the most ungodly, piercing scream I had ever heard. It was the same sound the demons had made the night before. In a second, everyone in the locker room was red-eyed and screeching.

I whirled around and raced out of there, slamming through the back door — and I ran straight into Zarkos, the masked wrestler. In a nanosecond he flipped me into the air, then pinned me on the ground in a wrestling hold.

"No fair!" I cried. "This doesn't count! I didn't have time to summon my *chi*!"

SHAGGY

 Scooby and I were still standing with Fred and his transformed pals when a terrible, horrible, hideous screaming came from somewhere behind the hotel. I remembered that Daphne was back there.

"Fred, did you hear that?" I asked.

He didn't seem to even hear me. He was staring at Scooby. "Get the dog," he said in a flat, expressionless voice.

Then his eyes turned bright red!

"Tell me this is part of the laser light show," I groaned.

Brad the Goth and the metal guy also turned all red-eyed. They jumped up on tables and did the same horrible scream I was hearing from the hotel. It was, like, the same scream the demons had made the other night.

Next, Sugar Ray started screaming and running toward us, their red eyes blazing.

Scoob and I had no idea how to handle this. I had only one thought. "Run!" I yelled.

We ran toward the back of the hotel. Then we spotted a wooden storage shack, so we headed for it. We raced inside and I slammed the bolt lock into position.

Scoob and I caught our breath. "Rhy is Red in a rad rood?" Scooby asked.

"That's no bad mood," I assured him. "Fred is possessed."

An arm smashed through the shack wall.

Scooby began to scream. But thankfully, it wasn't a freaky scream. It was pure, normal terror.

The band had climbed to the roof and they were using their guitars like axes to chop their way into the shack. The other possessed humans were tearing away the shack's planks. And all the while they kept up that horrible, scary screeching.

It looked like this was, like, it. We were captured for sure. I just covered my face, waiting for the end.

Scooby tapped my shoulder. When I opened

my eyes I saw that he'd put on a helmet and goggles. He pointed to the corner of the shack where two motorcycles sat, the keys still in the ignition switches.

I grabbed a helmet and goggles off a shelf and jumped onto a motorcycle. Scoob and I blasted out of that shack, sending wood splinters flying. It didn't take long before we left those howling weirdos behind.

We were zooming down Nightmare Boulevard, part of the amusement park, when I heard a woman scream. Mary Jane staggered into my path. I slammed on the brakes, skidding to a stop in front of her.

"I just saw my friend Bethanne," she cried breathlessly. "Something's wrong with her eyes. They're red!"

"Like, hop on!" I told her. She got onto the back of the motorcycle and wrapped her arms around my waist. I gunned the motor and caught up with Scooby, who had gotten ahead of me.

Looking behind, I saw the new, cleaned-up Brad the Goth running toward us. He was falling farther and farther behind, though. We were too fast for them.

I wanted to put some real distance between those screamers and us. I went even faster, swerving around corners and jumping over rocks.

I ducked to get past a low hanging branch. I heard something bang. Had Mary Jane been hit with the branch? "You okay?" I shouted.

She didn't answer. I was afraid to turn around and check on her — I didn't want to drive off the road. So I figured I'd better stop and see what was happening. It just happened that we were right by that strange platform we'd seen the night before, the one with the big face with the horns and mouth.

As I was turning to check on Mary Jane, Scooby pulled up beside me. He began barking crazily.

I'm probably the only one on earth who knows what Scooby is saying when he's all excited like that. But even I couldn't believe what he was saying.

He was trying to tell me that the branch hit Mary Jane and knocked her mask off. "Like, what do you mean — there's a Mary Jane mask?" I questioned him.

He said that, like, underneath her face was a monster face. He claimed she'd been able to pull her face back on just as I pulled off the road. Poor Scooby — he was so jealous of the special closeness Mary Jane and I shared that I guess he'd say anything to break us up.

"Man, I can't believe you'd stoop so low!" I yelled at him.

He barked at me, calling me some names I didn't exactly appreciate. "Oh, yeah?" I shouted, jumping off my quad-runner. "Maybe you'd like a taste of the Shagster!"

We circled each other, both of us with our fists in the air. We kept moving as we circled. Somehow we managed to step onto the platform, still circling. Before long we were over by the big mouth entry. But I barely even noticed that, I was so mad.

Then, the big mouth suddenly opened, swallowing Scooby! I could hear his howl echoing as though he were falling down a long tunnel.

I had to get in there to save him. Mary Jane ran onto the platform. "Scooby's been eaten," I told her quickly. "Go hide. I'll be right back."

"But, Shaggy, it's too dangerous," she argued.

The mouth was starting to slide closed. "I've got to!" I shouted as I dove down into the closing wall just in time.

I found myself sliding down a long, twisting tube. It let me out into a big warehouse of a room with very high ceilings. Along the sides of the room, many tunnels led in different directions.

Scooby barked, and the sound of it echoed around the cavernous space. I couldn't tell which tunnel he was in. He barked again, but it was no use. There was no way to tell where he was, so I just picked a tunnel and started walking down it. "Scooby-Doo, where are you?" I called as I went.

I turned a corner and — yikes! — I came face-to-face with a monster. I leaped back. Then I saw it was just a big mask. There were all kinds of native robes, grass skirts, fake teeth necklaces, sandals, and stuff hung on hooks all around.

I kept going, turned a corner, then stopped. I had come to a room even bigger and higher than the first one. Eight vertical wooden slabs encircled a big iron-and-glass vat in the middle of the room. Whatever the vat held, it was throwing wild green light out of the top.

"I call redo! Let me out!" someone shouted. Looking more closely, I saw that Daphne was strapped onto one of the wooden slabs. Three of the possessed college kids walked around her as if they hadn't heard her.

Zarkos walked into the room from another door. He climbed a long metal staircase and went into some kind of control booth at the top of it. As he did this, one of his native-dressed henchmen dug the Daemon Ritus out of Daphne's purse, which lay on the floor.

He stuck it into the controls of a machine that looked something like a crane. It was an upright metal device with an enormous pincer on the end. The henchman turned the Daemon Ritus, and the machine began to move.

I saw that Zarkos was controlling it from up in his control room. He worked levers as the pincer slowly moved toward Daphne.

"Nooooo!" Daphne shrieked in terror.

I wanted to help her, but I didn't know what to do. I could only watch, horrified, as the pincer moved *into* Daphne's chest. She screamed, but she didn't seem to be hurt. The pincer seemed to move magically into her without creating a wound. The pincer glowed as it twisted and dug inside her. It appeared to be searching for something.

It must have found what it was looking for, because Daphne suddenly fell limp.

I clamped my hand over my mouth, horrified. Had that thing, like, killed her?

But then I heard something *really* strange. Daphne's voice. Her body still lay there, lifeless.

But, from somewhere, she spoke. I couldn't tell exactly what she was saying, but she was definitely speaking.

Then things got even weirder.

The pincer moved back out of her chest, yanking something out with it. That something was white and glowed. It was, like, a ghost. The pincer seemed to draw it out of Daphne like warm taffy through a pinhole. When it was all finally out, I could see Daphne's head attached to a wispy, spiny tail. It was, like, her *soul* or something.

The ghostly Daphne looked down at her own limp body. "What the —?" Now that she was out of her body, I could hear Daphne's soul speak much more clearly. "You're taking my soul out of my body? That is so uncool!"

One of the horrible demons from the night before appeared, seeming to pop up out of nowhere. Moving quickly, he shoved his head into Daphne's mouth.

It was such a horrible sight that I had to turn away. When I got the nerve to look again, I saw only the demon's foot hanging out of Daphne's mouth. In another second, that, too, was gone. It was hideous. The entire demon was now inside Daphne.

Meanwhile, the pincer held tight to Daphne's freaked-out soul. It swung her over to the vat and stuffed her into the mix.

At the same time, the eyes in Daphne's body snapped open. Possessed college kids undid her straps. She now stood straight and moved her neck and her joints, trying to get used to this new body. *"Ak orton. Blaknoerpa,"* she said to one of the possessed ones.

I leaned back hard against the wall of my tunnel. This had to be some sort of nightmare. It couldn't be real. But it was. And I had to do something about it.

Peering around the corner again, I saw Daphne leave with the other possessed ones. Zarkos wasn't in the control room any longer, either. This was my chance to see what was in that glowing vat.

I crept along the walls in the room, keeping to the shadows. No one seemed to be around, so I ran up the steps leading to the vat. I gazed down into the swirling brew. "Zoinks!" I cried.

Inside the vat were hundreds of swirling faces. They were white and see-through, just like Daphne's soul-face had been. The sound they made was seriously spooky — screaming, whispering, teeth chattering.

I spotted a familiar face. Not Daphne, but Velma. She swirled past me. "Shaggy!" she cried.

Even though I was scared, I tried not to think about it. I plunged my arm into the vat and grabbed at Velma's moving soul as it swirled around past me again.

I got it!

Velma's soul flew up into the air. For a minute I thought she was going to, like, lift me up with her. "Shaggy! Let go," she said. "I have a feeling I'll return to my body. And then you get out of here before they find you and steal your soul, too."

I wasn't sure it was the right thing to do, but I released her hand. She shot away from me and out of the room in a streak of light.

Looking back into the vat, I saw Fred's soul swirl by and grabbed him by the end of his spiny tail. He was, like, majorly freaked.

"Listen, man! Someone must have spiked my root beer last night! Talk me down, pal," he babbled.

I looked around quickly. I didn't want his loud voice to attract anyone's attention. "Shhh!" I said. "A demon took over your body."

"A demon?" Fred said, sounding pretty doubtful. "Shaggy, cut the superstitious claptrap! At the end of every paranormal claim there are only fools seeking power and —"

"Fred, you're a see-through protoplasmic head!" I whispered harshly.

Fred frowned. "Um . . . well, I'm the best-looking protoplasmic head here, right?" Then Fred flew off in a streak of light just like Velma had.

It took me a while to find Daphne's face. Finally, though, I spotted her and snapped her up. I expected at least a little thanks. But, instead, she was steamed. "Put me back, Shaggy," she scolded. "I don't want to be saved again. I'll figure a way out myself."

"Like, how?" I asked.

"I'll . . . I don't know, use my tongue as an oar to paddle to the edge."

"Forget it, Daphne," I said, tossing her into the air. "Go find your body!"

Daphne sped out of the room, just like Fred and Velma had. I felt sorry for the other souls in the vat. Once we'd solved the case, we'd come back and free them all. Right now, there just wasn't time to, like, pull them all out.

I climbed down the stairs, remembering that the Daemon Ritus was still in the soul-snatching pincer machine. Now we knew why it was so important. The machine couldn't work without it. I had to get it back so they couldn't steal any more souls.

The evil pyramid came loose with one strong tug. "Gotcha!" I said. My next step was to find my way out of this room. Looking around at all the tunnels, I realized it might not be so easy.

VELMA

There was no doubt that this was — by far — the strangest thing that had ever happened to me. I was me, with my personality, my mind, my feelings, but without my body. And without my glasses, too, I should add. Everything was a blur.

But my soul was guided by some irresistible pull toward my body. I flew through the air at amazing speed. My soul raced straight to the spooky castle. I zapped down some dark hallways. Then I saw an orange blur. Somehow I just knew it was me — the possessed me, that is.

Whap! I slammed right into myself, knocking myself off my feet. In a second I was inside.

But I wasn't alone.

The demon inside me screamed. He tried to scare me out, but it didn't work. I was home and there was no room for the two of us. I gave him a kick to show him who was boss. A second kick sent him flying out of my chest.

I found my glasses in my skirt pocket and things became clear — a little too clear. I was staring right up at this gigantic demon that was glaring at me with furious red eyes. *Jinkies*, I thought. *Now what am I going to do with tall, gruesome, and angry here?*

A beam of sunlight shone through a window high above us. It hit the demon's body and — *pppffffwap!* — the demon exploded into glowing protoplasmic chunks.

It was really gross. I was covered in the horrible stuff. But, in seconds, it shriveled and disappeared. I shivered as I wiped the last of it from my glasses. At least I was alive.

I looked around. There was no one nearby. No one knew yet that I wasn't possessed anymore. I wondered if Shaggy had been able to find Fred's and Daphne's souls. Then I looked out a window and saw a streak of white light in the forest. I couldn't see exactly who it was. I had the idea that it looked like Daphne, though.

I had to help Daphne connect with her spirit. I saw the possessed Daphne walking toward me down the hall. What if her soul couldn't get into the castle? I'd found my way in through an open door, but I didn't know if Daphne would find it.

I had an idea. I opened the window beside me. Then I hung out next to it. I smiled at Daphne's possessed body as it came near, then I grabbed her arm and pushed up against the window. I saw the light head straight in through the window and fly into Daphne's face.

Score!

An enormous demon popped out of her chest. Only this one didn't explode. The sun had moved.

The demon grabbed Daphne by the throat and slammed her up against the wall. This was bad!

I grabbed the half-shut shade and pulled the cord. "I think you need a little light," I said. When I released it, the shade snapped all the way up, lighting the shadowy hall.

Snap! Crackle! Pop! One less demon.

Daphne stared at me, wide-eyed and confused.

"That's one part of the mystery solved," I told her. "The demons must need our bodies to survive in sunlight. Like a human suit — SPF one million. But why are they here in the first place?"

Daphne nodded, though she still seemed seriously stunned. It was as though she couldn't get over the shock of what had happened to her.

That was something I certainly understood. The whole thing was pretty hard to believe. "I'm all right, but I'm not Daphne," she answered in a voice that was definitely male.

"Fred?" I asked.

Daphne's head nodded. "Yeah," Fred's voice replied. "I couldn't get to my body. I was almost there, when my possessed body slammed the door. I bounced off the door like a volleyball and flew out a window. I didn't know where else to go. It's difficult to steer when you're pure spirit. Then I saw Daphne, so I hopped in."

I didn't know how we would fix that situation. In all my reading and research I'd never found anything about soul swapping.

I was distracted by the open door next to Daphne/Fred. Behind the door was an office. There was nothing odd about it except that a gigantic world map hung on the wall behind the desk. Pegs were clustered around various cities.

I gestured for Daphne/Fred to follow me into the office. Going up to the map, I studied it. Under the map was a wire with a nub end attached to it. The end piece seemed to plug into something. On a hunch, I took the wire and tried to plug it into a peg stuck into the city of Washington, D.C.

On the wall to my right, a huge photo of a young woman appeared. An electronic voice boomed from a speaker over the map. "Moira Murphy. Host to Arkaeovven. Visited Spooky World 1998. Senator's Aide, Washington, D.C."

I moved the peg and placed it on a peg at St. Louis, Missouri. The picture changed to that of a young man. "Andre Cozine. Host to Blorgtrrl," the electronic voice reported. "Visited Spooky Island 2001. Police officer, St. Louis, Missouri."

I turned to Daphne/Fred. "People come to Spooky Island, the demons possess their bodies, and they go out all over America."

Daphne nodded and replied in Fred's voice, "And they all seem to be getting jobs with government agencies, which leads me to believe this conspiracy extends far beyond Spooky Island."

I smiled at him. Maybe I'd underestimated Fred's brainpower. "Good detective work, Fred," I complimented him.

Fred seemed alarmed by my words. "Oh, wow!"

"What?" I asked.

"I'm piecing things together so much faster with Daphne's brain," Fred's voice explained.

DAPHNE

This was unbelievable! My soul was zooming toward my body, pulled by an indescribable force. We were about to be re-united and everything would have been fine.

And then that idiot Fred stepped right in front of me. Or, I should say Fred's possessed body. It stepped right out into the hall.

Slam!

I smashed right into him. And I do mean *in* — right into Fred's chest. One of those hideous demons came popping out and stepped into a beam of sunlight streaming in from the window. Instantly, he shriveled into disgusting chunks.

The demon exploding was cool, but now I had a really big problem. I was inside Fred! It was terrible. I had to find a way out.

I had absolutely no idea what to do, so I went

out into the woods to look for the gang. It didn't take long before I found Velma and . . . well, me.

"Daphne, are you in there?" Velma asked.

"Yes," I said. "Who's in me?"

"I am," Fred's voice answered. From my body!

It was too freaky. I couldn't take it. "Well, get out!" I shouted.

Just then Shaggy came trooping through the trees. When he saw us, he jumped behind a tree. Slowly, he peeked around it. "Please tell me you're you," he whimpered.

"We're us, sort of," Velma replied.

Shaggy seemed convinced. He came out from behind the tree. He pulled the Daemon Ritus from beneath his shirt and held it out. "I got this. Maybe it can help us," he said.

The moment Shaggy held up the pyramid, all four of our souls blasted out of our mouths. Once again I was a bodiless soul hovering over the four limp bodies below. We swirled, spun, and then returned to our bodies.

"I'm me again!" I cried, thrilled to be back.

"Yippee for you," Velma snapped irritably. It was Velma's voice, anyway. But it was coming out of Fred's body. "Fred," she said. "How can you stand your pants being so tight?"

The next voice I heard belonged to Shaggy — only it came from Velma's body. "Like, why am I wearing a skirt?" he asked, looking down.

Fred's voice came out of Shaggy's body. "Everyone remain calm," he said. He turned to his own body. "Velma! What the heck is going on?"

Velma spoke from Fred's mouth. "If my calculations are correct," she began, "due to the fragile nature of unstable soul quarks in the proximity of the Daemon Ritus, we're simply going to continue randomly changing until —"

She was interrupted by another wave of body switching. All our souls flew up another time, swirled, and landed back in completely different bodies.

"— until the souls are aligned with the right bodies," Velma finished wearily.

I looked down at my big feet and saw that I was Fred again. I wanted to scream.

Shaggy's voice came out of my body. "What's wrong with you, Daphne? Don't you eat anything? I'm going to faint."

"Look, I think there may be a way to speed this up," Velma spoke out of Shaggy's mouth. "Shaggy, Fred, quick! Cover your mouths."

I looked at her, confused. What did she have in mind?

Shaggy/Velma blew in my face. Our spirits switched. We kept switching, some of us covering our mouths, some blowing on each other, until we were all back where we belonged.

"I'm me!" Fred cried in his own voice.

"Like, me too," Shaggy said, sounding like himself.

I was definitely myself again and that meant Velma was, too. She grabbed the Daemon Ritus and began examining it carefully. "I need to figure out what's going on here," she explained. She looked up at Shaggy. "Where's Scooby?"

"He was eaten," Shaggy said. "It's all my fault."

Fred went pale at Shaggy's words. "You *ate* Scooby? Good god, man! We were only gone for a day. Just how far do your munchies go?"

We all just stared at Fred. He could be unbelievably stupid sometimes.

"We've got to find Scooby," Shaggy said desperately.

Suddenly, something exploded! We saw the flames blazing through the trees. It seemed to have come from the beach.

"Come on, gang," I shouted as I began running through the trees toward the beach. I ran, with the gang behind me, leaping over fallen branches and underbrush. The Voodoo Maestro was ahead of me. He was charred and tattered from the explosion.

"Follow him!" I told the gang. He didn't know we were there, so we managed to follow him through the trees. He kept running until he came to a flaming pit of stones.

I felt sure of myself, in command. "I know how to handle this guy," I told the gang. I called up to the voodoo guy. "Hey, you! What are you doing?"

He began speaking, but I couldn't tell if he was talking to himself or to me. He seemed like a man on a mission, half crazed with fear and determined to accomplish whatever it was he was doing. "A voodoo ritual with various ingredients," he mumbled, "eye of newt, wing of bat, witch's fire, aerosol hairspray. The only way I can protect myself from the demons is by blessing this dead arnouki beast."

We gazed at the hideous animal spinning on a stick over the fire. I'd never seen anything like it. It was a disgusting animal, veiny and rotten, with diseased bulbous eyes. We all stepped back, horrified. All of us except Shaggy, that is. "Are you, like, going to eat that?" he asked hungrily.

"Shaggy!" Velma cried in disbelief.

Shaggy shrugged. "I'm starving."

"Who are you?" I asked the Voodoo Maestro.

The Voodoo Maestro whirled around and stared at me with burning eyes. "I'm the last real native on this island. There's always been weird things going on here, but lately, someone over at the amusement park has actually been summoning demons! I've only got a little time to stop them from performing their evil Darkopolypse ritual."

Velma suddenly cried out in surprise. I turned and saw that she'd turned the Daemon Ritus and opened it. She pointed to some writing inside it.

"Darkopolypse ritual!" she said excitedly. "That's what this ancient text describes!" She began reading. "There's a dance and an incantation," she reported. "You need an offering of five thousand souls as an energy source."

It suddenly hit me! "That's what the souls in the vat are for!"

Velma kept reading. "And an imperfect soul needs to absorb a purely good soul."

The Voodoo Maestro had moved close to Velma and stared intently at the Daemon Ritus. "Legend has it that once the Darkopolypse is performed, demons will rule Earth for ten thousand years."

Ten thousand years? Demons? Oh, this was really, really bad!

"I'm taking my arnouki beast home," the Voodoo Maestro stated, sounding panicky, "where I can protect myself without any ghost-hunting, *Dawson's Creek*–looking namby-pambies mucking things up!" He then grabbed his flaming stick with the horrible animal attached and walked off in the direction of his shack.

I was so upset by what I'd just heard. "Demons are taking over the world!" I said. "That's so mean!" Strange as it sounded, it sure made sense. "That's why all the possessed humans are in the government offices — they're covering up any hint of conspiracy!"

"Wait!" Fred cried. "They can't do the ritual without a pure human soul. Where in the world are they going to get that?"

"I didn't say *human*," Velma corrected him. We all stared at one another. Scooby!

"Oh, boy," Shaggy said, turning pale.

Velma continued, "So, if the person behind all this needs Scooby's soul —"

"— then that person is the one who brought Scooby here!" I realized.

SCOOBY

Rafter ri rell rough re roor, ri ras ry ryself ror ra rittle rhile. Ren ri rell rasleep. Ren ri roke up, ri ras rack rin rhe rotel. Rut ri rasn't ralone ranymore.

"Scoobert!" raid Rondavarious. "How are you, my friend?"

Re ras reating rog rood from a rowl. Rit rooked relicious! Rhen ri roticed rere ras ra ricture of re ron ris resk. "Hey! Rat's re!"

Rondavarious raughed. "It certainly is. That's because — why? — we love you, Scooby-Doo. Unlike that alleged friend of yours, Shaggy. He wouldn't believe you about that nasty girl, Mary Jane, would he?"

Ri rook ry read. Raggy rad reen ro rean ro re! Ri rought re ras ry riend.

"Well, I believe you, my friend," raid Rondavarious. "And that's why I have a very important job for you. Scooby, I'd like you to be a *sacrifice*."

"Rhat? Re?" Ri rasked. Rondavarious rodded. "A *racrifice*?" Ri rouldn't relieve row rucky I ras. Ri rad a rew riend, Rondavarious, and re ranted re to re a *racrifice*! Raggy rad rever rasked re to ro *rhat*.

VELMA

Suddenly, all the pieces clicked into place. It all made sense.

"But that doesn't make sense," Fred said. "If Mondorajagaga only needed Scooby, why did he invite the rest of us?"

"It doesn't matter, man!" Shaggy said, sounding shaky and scared. "We have to go, like, save Scoob!"

Oh, god. I was so scared. Solving mysteries and unmasking bad guys in costumes was one thing. But these monsters were for real!

"Shag, our area of expertise is nut jobs in costumes!" Fred objected.

"We're supposed to be heroes!" Shaggy shouted at him.

I had to tell the truth. "I'm too scared to be a hero," I said.

Shaggy threw his arms out to his sides and

began pacing, ranting as he went. "I was so scared the time when Chickenstein jumped at me out of that giant coop, but I still went back for Daphne."

"Chickenstein wasn't real," Daphne reminded him.

"They've all been real to me, man!" Shaggy shouted. "So I'm going to do what I always do."

He suddenly snapped up Daphne's purse and pulled out the box of Scooby Snacks we always keep in case of emergencies. "I'm gonna eat myself a Scooby Snack and then I'm going to save my best pal." He gobbled one down, then held out the box to me.

Oh, no. "Velmster?" Fred asked.

"You think I'm going to fall for that? Giving me my own nickname? Trying to make me feel like . . . part of the gang?" For a minute, I thought I was going to cry. Then I pulled myself together. We had to save Scooby. "We could make a plan."

Daphne looked near tears, too. "But what can *I* do? All I'm good for is getting caught."

Fred put his hand on her shoulder. "But you've never let that stop you, Daph. If that's not a true hero, I don't know what is." He took a Scooby Snack from the box, then passed it to Daphne. She took one.

We all ate one. I'd never had a Scooby Snack before and now I felt ... like I was about to vomit. But the feeling of togetherness, being one with the gang again, was wonderful.

Shaggy put out his hand. Fred, Daphne, and I put our hands on top of his. "Let's get jinky with it!" I shouted.

FRED

I felt that old rush of excitement. We were at my favorite part of every case — the plan!

"To achieve our goal, we'll need a light-refracting device," Velma said. We'd assembled in Dead Mike's to prepare.

I spotted a skull-shaped disco ball in a corner. I waved to Shaggy to help me carry it out.

"And some rappelling gear," Velma continued.

Daphne joined in. "We'll create a diversion and infiltrate the cavern."

I offered my bit. "Once inside, we'll hang this disco skull —"

"— and use neo-Newtonian physics to create a complex series of pulleys," Velma finished.

"Okay," I continued. "So we use the pulleys to tip over the vat, and the souls are freed."

"Correct," Daphne said. "The demons will run in to see what happened."

"At which point, Daphne will open the air vents up top and release the disco skull. The light will refract from the skull," I explained.

"The demons will explode!" Shaggy went on. "I'll find Scooby and we'll have, like, saved the world."

I felt pretty proud of myself. I hadn't hogged up all the planning and the leadership. I'd allowed everyone to have their say. This was teamwork like never before.

Together, we made our way to the castle. We stayed back, hidden in the bushes, while Shaggy created the distraction.

He approached the two guards, walking his funkiest walk and talking like the possessed humans. "Yo! That's the stylin' new retro freestyle old-school face Mondavarious wants you to practice at the Ring of Fire nizznow."

Shaggy did such a good job that the guards twisted their faces to look like Shaggy's, then they ran right off toward the beach to practice. The moment they were gone, we all scurried inside and found our way through a tunnel and back to the huge room that held the vat of souls.

Daphne and I used the rappelling ropes to

suspend ourselves from the ceiling and hang the disco skull. Shaggy and Velma set up the pulleys as we'd planned.

We were just about done when I heard the sound of distant drumming. "Oh, no!" I cried. "The ritual's beginning!"

We joined Velma, who stood up on the iron platform. Daphne climbed over the side railing and hung from her rope, her pick holding her to the side of the wall.

Velma quickly lowered the last bit of rope to Shaggy down on the floor by the vat of souls. "Shaggy, attach this to the vat," she directed. "Hurry!"

Shaggy raced to the vat and began clasping on the rope. Despite the danger, I felt excited and happy in a way I hadn't felt since our last case.

"If this works, it could be even cooler than the time we kicked Dick Van Dyke's butt with the Cotton Candy Ghost." I whispered to Velma.

"You mean the time we kicked the Cotton Candy Ghost's butt with Dick Van Dyke."

I looked at her doubtfully. "Are you sure? 'Cause I remember putting the hurt on Van Dyke."

From somewhere inside the castle I could

hear voices chanting. The scary low drone seemed to be coming closer. I realized they were inside one of the tunnels.

"Faster, Shaggy," Velma urged.

He finished attaching the rope to the vat. "Okay! Go! Go!" he called to us.

Velma and I grabbed onto our end of the rope and pulled. There was only one problem.

Shaggy had goofed! He'd attached his end of the rope to his belt instead of to the vat!

Velma's and my combined weight sent Shaggy flying into the air. He slammed into the ceiling and dislodged the central pulley. Then he flew across the room and crashed down into a dark corner.

Daphne was still hanging on her rappelling rope, her pick point in the wall. But when Shaggy flew by, he smacked into her and knocked her pick out of the wall. She went swinging across the room. She hit a high, rocky ledge and her support rope fell away. She clung to the ledge, not daring to look down.

And that was when Mondavarious and N'goo came in. Mondavarious was now dressed in royal robes with some kind of strange metal plate on the front of his chest. His henchmen followed, along with a group of skeleton warriors. Possessed humans came in after them.

Velma and I crouched down together on the metal platform. We shoved the pulleys behind us, hopefully out of sight. This plan hadn't exactly been our most successful. "Life on Earth is screwed," I whispered to Velma. "Darn! Double darn!"

I saw Daphne still dangling from the ledge. "I've got to save Daphne," I said.

"No! You'll expose us all," Velma disagreed. "She'll be okay. Act like you're possessed."

"What?" I asked. Velma's eyes glazed over like the eyes of the possessed college kids. "Oh, that's disturbing," I muttered. But she was right. Fooling Mondavarious and N'goo into thinking we were still possessed was our only hope now. I tried my best to make my eyes look glazed.

With my heart pounding, I got up and followed Velma down the stairs to join the possessed college kids.

SHAGGY

Zoinks! My head sure hurt. I'd crashed really hard into a corner. I felt like a major jerk. How could I have hooked that rope into my pants? I guess I was nervous.

I peeked around a corner into the room. I saw a henchman in a hideous mask open a door. Scooby was carried in through the door on a golden plank. A wreath of flowers hung around his ears. Beautiful, possessed women fed him Scooby Snacks. He didn't seem too upset. In fact, my old pal was loving it.

Looking up, I saw that Daphne had managed to climb up onto a ledge. She squeezed into a vent, and I lost sight of her.

All the possessed humans were, like, hanging around. I saw Brad the Goth, the heavy-metal guy, Melvin Doo, and the bartender from Dead

Mike's. They began chanting and started doing a dance.

It was a dance with steps and they all seemed to know them, like a demonic macarena. The only two who didn't know the steps were Velma and Fred.

They had no choice but to try to dance along with the others. "*A ringio a wado set!*" the possessed ones chanted. "*Ba bingam tom anani fett! Ree kimio an rako ling!* This is what we demons sing!"

Fred and Velma tried to sing along. "*La banana fana fofana, me my momana!* This is the thing we say."

The chanting slowly stopped as the possessed humans realized that, like, Velma and Fred weren't exactly with the program. Fred shot them a nervous smile. "Yo! Yo! Uh, dudes, you forgot the last part," Fred tried to bluff his way through. "You forgot the part where we do the Electric Slide. See?"

Fred started to do the Slide. He slid his way back toward one of the tunnels. He took hold of Velma's wrist and drew her back with him.

For a minute, I thought they'd get away with it. Then two henchmen grabbed them. One of them dug through Velma's backpack and pulled out the Daemon Ritus.

Mondavarious hurried up to them, his royal robes dragging behind his skinny self. "Ah, yes, Fred, Velma," he said in a smirking voice. "Welcome to my little end-of-the-world party. You pathetic sods!"

This guy was really getting me, like, mad! Sure he was a villain, but did he have to be so insulting?

Mondavarious kept going with his little speech to Fred and Velma. "You never *solved* mysteries. You simply stumbled blindly into the obvious. Just as I knew you'd stumble back here and bring the only missing piece of my master plan. The Daemon Ritus!"

One of his henchmen walked up to Mondavarious and pressed the pyramid onto the metal plate on his chest. When Mondavarious looked down at it, his eyes brightened with excitement.

"My children, the hour of the Darkopolypse is upon us!" he shouted. "Bring forth the pure soul. Behold, it should be . . . the sacrifice!"

The possessed college kids started chanting again. This time it was even louder and more frenzied. Dancers in, like, strange native-type outfits led a parade. Behind them were henchmen in masks. They carried the stretcher with Scooby on it. He still didn't look too concerned. The glass vase of Scooby Snacks at his side was keeping him busy.

The chant grew louder still. *"A hinga hoowa karay lun. Bolevven taray pakin tun. Ropoppo ee en loo en roo.* Offer praise to Scooby-Doo!"

I'm not usually the one who comes up with the plan. But the usual planners were now in deep trouble — and so was my pal Scooby. I remembered that I'd seen those masks the other day when I went through the tunnel.

For the first time ever — I had a plan!

I kept low and crept along the wall. Luck was on my side. Everyone was so, like, interested in Scooby and their chant that no one noticed me. I got to the tunnel and pulled on a mask and some of that funky native-style stuff. Then I came back looking like one of Mondavarious's henchmen. I joined the parade circling the big room.

When I neared Velma and Fred, I lifted my mask quickly to let them know it was me. Fred was looking away, but Velma saw me.

The possessed college kids were chanting so

loudly that I was able to speak to Scooby-Doo without being heard. "Psst," I said as I came up alongside him.

He turned toward me. "Raggy?"

"Scoob, let's run for it! We've, like, got to get out of here!" I whispered.

Scooby shook his head. "Ruh-uh!" He pointed to himself proudly. "Ri'm a racrifice."

"A sacrifice!" I whispered harshly. "Dude! That's not a good thing! Listen, I'm sorry I yelled at you. I haven't been a very good friend since we got here. But you've got to trust me now."

"Roo ron't rust re," he argued.

This was crazy. I couldn't believe he was arguing about this. Did he want to be sacrificed? Did he even understand what was going on here? "I do trust you," I insisted as I kept moving alongside Scooby and his royal stretcher.

"Raryrane's a ran in a rask!" he said.

"She's not a man in a mask!" I said, louder than I meant to. "She just has some allergies. Now, come on, who's your best buddy?"

I couldn't believe it, but Scooby seemed to need time to think about the answer to this question. "Raggy," he finally admitted.

"That's right!" I said. "And who's *my* best buddy?"

"Rooby-Doo," Scooby said.

"Yes, sir!" I agreed. "Me and you! We're trippy peas in a far-out pod! And best buddies trust each other. So, let's do what we do best — run out of here, screaming like a couple of lunatics."

Scooby smiled and nodded. His long tongue dangled enthusiastically.

"On the count of five," I began. "One . . . two . . ."

But before I got to three, the soul-snatcher machine slammed down into Scooby's body!

"Scooby!" I shouted. I looked up at the iron platform. N'goo was in the control room, working the levers.

Mondavarious stood in front of Scooby. The Daemon Ritus flipped down, revealing a, like, scary, huge hole in his chest.

The pincer twisted and yanked out Scooby's soul. His body slumped over as his confused soul was pulled away by the soul snatcher. "Raggy?" Scooby's soul called to me sadly. He didn't know what was going on. He needed my help. But what could I do for him now?

The pincer lifted Scooby's soul over the vat of stolen souls. The souls began churning, spinning in a circle. I could hear their screams. It was horrible.

A cold wind swept through the cavernous room. Like water swirling down a drain, the souls began to be sucked up out of the vat, through the air, through the Daemon Ritus, and into Mondavarious's chest.

Mondavarious's body began to pulse as he absorbed the power of, like, five thousand souls. "Now to complete the transformation!" he yelled triumphantly. "I shall absorb the pure soul! Ultimate power shall be mine!"

That's what he thought! "No one absorbs my pal!" I shouted. I took a deep breath and leaped onto the soul snatcher. The evil machine went, like, crazy, rolling out of control. The pincer swung around and crashed into Mondavarious. It sent him flying to the ground. The souls stopped pouring into him.

I wondered how the possessed crowd would react to all this, but they were in some kind of mesmerized trance. They just stood there looking dazed.

My evil pal N'goo struggled like crazy to regain control of the soul snatcher. He pushed buttons and pulled levers like a wild man. The pincer swung around again, and Scooby's soul was shaken free. It ricocheted around the room in a frenzy.

FRED

Mondavarious's henchmen kept Velma and me in a tight grip. But they were distracted when Scooby's soul started flying around the room.

That was our chance! Velma and I broke loose from their grip. We raced over to Mondavarious, who lay spread out on the floor. I looked down at him and found exactly what I was looking for. A small tear around his neck. "Look, Velma, a man in a mask." I reached down and stuck my hand into the tear. With that faint, familiar tearing sound, the mask came off.

"Jinkies!" Velma cried as a robotic face was revealed beneath the latex mask. Electric sparks began snapping around Mondavarious's body. His chest began to crack open. Something was starting to come out of it!

"Scrappy-Doo!" I shouted. I couldn't believe

what I was seeing. It was Scooby's pesky nephew, all right. I'd know him anywhere. He was wearing a biomechanical suit that made him seem to be a human body with a Scrappy head.

"Who's been spiking his Alpo?" Velma gasped.

The Daemon Ritus remained attached to Scrappy's chest. I figured I'd better get it before he could use it to cause any more trouble. But as I reached out to grab it, Scrappy's body began to throb and pulse. His nostrils flared and his eyes turned dark. His voice grew deeper, and he began to grow up and out of the suit.

"I, Scrappy-Dappy-Doo, shall inherit the promise of the Daemon Ritus and the power of the Darkopolypse!" he thundered, his voice booming in the huge room. "I will rule the world with a demon army at my command. And I've brought you here — puny, pathetic Mystery, Inc. — to witness my moment of triumph. I will rock you and sock you and crush you like bugs! All I need to complete my plan is —"

He whirled around and pointed at Scooby. "YOU!!"

Scooby looked around, then pointed to himself. "Re?" Then he pointed to Melvin Doo, who was standing beside him. "Ron't rou rean *rim*?"

"Seize them!" Scrappy screamed.

Henchmen ran to all the exits, blocking them. Slowly, they closed in on us. Scrappy used his supersized fist to slam Velma and me into the wall. Ow!

"This is totally ungroovyyyyyy!" Shaggy shouted as he and Scooby took off running. Henchmen chased them as they dodged through a human forest of possessed college kids.

Velma and I dusted ourselves off, recovering from our crash landing. "Scrappy is still wearing the Daemon Ritus," I told Velma. "What are we going to do now?"

"We've got to tip the soul vat," Velma replied.

"How?" I asked.

Velma gazed up at N'goo, who was still manning the soul pincer. "The pincer," she said.

She and I raced up the metal stairs. Velma ran for N'goo in the control room, but she was instantly blocked by a horde of henchmen.

I was able to scoop up the rope and pulleys we'd stashed earlier. "Step back, bro-has. 'Cause Fredster's got his groove on!" I shouted as I swung the rope and pulley into an arm-wide circle. I swung that rope and pulley like a sideways lasso, knocking out one henchmen, then the next, then the next, with the metal pulley.

Below me I could see that gigantic Scrappy was about to grab Scooby!

Shaggy hung off the edge of the platform and yanked Scooby's tail. He pulled him away from Scrappy — for the moment.

Shaggy and Scooby huddled together on a small ledge beneath the iron platform. Scrappy swiped at them with his giant paw. He couldn't quite reach them, but he was only inches away.

Velma was at the control room booth, trying to open the door. It was locked. She threw things at it, trying to break the glass, but it was made of some kind of unbreakable material. Henchmen were running to stop her, but I kept heading them off and hitting them with a swinging pulley.

Meanwhile, I checked on Scooby and Shaggy. I wanted to go help them, but the henchmen kept coming.

Glancing down, I realized that there was now a third person on the ledge with Scooby and Shaggy. It was Mary Jane, the girl Shaggy was so gone over.

Then I saw something I never expected. Mary Jane grabbed Scooby and Shaggy by the necks and slammed them against the wall. She had superhuman strength — obviously she was one of *them*!

Still holding them by their necks, Mary Jane handed Scooby and Shaggy to Scrappy.

Scrappy raised his arm and looked up to N'goo, who was still in the control room. "Remove his pure soul! Now!" Scrappy roared.

N'goo pulled a lever, and the giant pincer began moving toward Scooby-Doo.

DAPHNE

 I crawled up through the vent and began climbing out onto the roof of the castle. I'd made it! Right away I started planning a way to get back down there and help my friends.

I didn't have long to think. Zarkos sneaked up from behind me and grabbed my ankles. I flipped into the air and fell hard on my back.

Not again! I told myself as I got to my feet. *He's not getting me again with his cheap wrestling tricks.* I quickly summoned my *chi* and prepared to fight.

Zarkos grabbed my neck in an iron fist. "Captured again, eh, senorita," he said with an infuriating, self-satisfied chuckle.

"No!" I cried, gasping for air. I shoved the palm of my hand hard up into his chin. As I'd planned, it knocked him back and I broke free.

"Not this time!" I shouted.

I shot him a swirling back kick that sent him stumbling back on the roof. He might have fallen off, except that he was able to cling to the vent opening. I couldn't give him time to make a counterattack.

I yanked him off the vent and flipped him over my shoulder. "Now who's the damsel in distress?!" I cried.

". . . Me?" Zarkos asked, sniveling.

"Straight up," I shot back. I released him, and he dropped and crashed through the vent, screaming as he tumbled down into the huge chamber below.

I felt something warm against my cheek and looked up. The sun! Of course. It was a beautiful, sunny day.

That was it!

VELMA

There had to be some way to get into that control room and commandeer that hideous soul-snatching machine. It looked to me like it was the only hope for Scooby now that Scrappy held Shaggy and him in his gigantic paws.

I saw a bobby pin on the floor and snapped it up. One thing I'm very good at is picking locks with a bobby pin. I knelt down in front of the door and worked until I heard something in the lock spring loose. N'goo was so busy with his controls that he didn't even notice me.

I wanted Fred to know that I had opened the door, but he was so busy with the henchmen that he didn't look my way. Then something hit me on the shoulder. It was a piece of wood. Looking up, I saw that Zarkos was falling through the air.

He'd crashed through the ceiling, and wood and glass were flying everywhere. Zarkos landed with a thud — right on top of the soul vat! It tipped over, and all the souls came flying out, filling the cavern.

Meanwhile, ceiling vents were opening. Someone on the roof was opening all the vents, sending rays of sunshine into the room.

Squinting against the sun and shielding my eyes, I saw Daphne moving around up there on the roof. Way to go, Daph! I saw her arm swing down through one of the vents as though she were searching for something.

The disco skull ball!

It hung from a rope, held up by the vents.

"Get it, Daphne, get it!" I said hopefully.

Yes! It swung down into the room, reflecting the sunlight that was now pouring in. Spots of light circled the room, bouncing all over.

All around the room, demons popped out of the chests of the possessed college kids as their souls returned to their bodies. As the demons came out, they instantly were struck by sunlight and exploded.

"Noooooo!" Scrappy screamed.

N'goo heard him scream and jumped up from

the controls. He went to the door, and it swung open as he touched it. In a second, Fred zoomed past me and clocked N'goo with a pulley.

N'goo fell to his knees, furious. "I'll rip out your heart!" he threatened Fred. "I'll get you!"

I jumped up and stepped in front of Fred. "The only thing you're getting is a Dinkley fist sandwich!"

I punched him once, then twice, and he fell over.

Fred stared at me, a look of awe on his face. I guess he didn't think I had it in me. I shrugged. "Guy *pet* my head earlier."

"Guess I'll remember not to do that," Fred said.

Fred and I ran outside the booth to see what was going on. Scrappy still held Scooby and Shaggy in his paws. Souls were racing all around them, returning to their original bodies.

Mary Jane's soul flew by. A demon popped out of her and burst into sparks and chunks of goo. She was able to reach out and grab Shaggy out of Scrappy's paw. But Scrappy still held on to Scooby.

Scrappy saw us on the platform and lunged in our direction, slamming his free paw down in front of us. We were trapped between the wall and his enormous paw.

"All my plans are destroyed!" he raged. "But I'll have my revenge on you! I'll rock you and sock you and crush you like bugs!"

I'll admit it — I was scared. So was Fred. I knew because he was shaking. Also because he was acting all sincere with Scrappy, trying to calm him down. "Scrapster, pal," he began in a calm, friendly voice. "A little rocking is okay. Even some socking may not be so bad. But crushing us like bugs? Come on. We used to be number-one buds."

Scrappy drew back his paw, getting ready to strike. "How's this for puppy power?" he threatened.

But just then, Scrappy was distracted by something. He turned, and I saw that the pincer of the soul snatcher was banging him on the back. A quick glance at the control room made me grin.

Shaggy was working the controls!

"Like, you're canceled, dude!" he shouted. The soul snatcher shot forward, slamming into the Daemon Ritus on Scrappy's chest. All the souls that had ever been sucked inside it came flying out in a greenish-white stream of glowing light. They zoomed around the room and streaked into the tunnels. They were headed for all the cities and towns where their bodies were now located. There would soon be a lot of government offices full of exploding demons.

With the Daemon Ritus smashed, Scrappy quickly shrank down to his original puny size. He tried to run for the door, but Scooby grabbed him by his collar, his little legs pumping helplessly in the air.

"Rotcha!" Scooby cried happily.

I turned to Fred and we smiled at each other. "Well, I guess that wraps up another mystery," he said.

My friend from the other night, the one I called Metal Head, ran up to me. I could tell from his smiling expression that he was back to his real self. He swept me off my feet and twirled me in a circle. I couldn't stop giggling, I was so happy!

Daphne rappelled down from the roof on a rope and punched Fred joyfully on the shoulder. "We did it!" she shouted. Fred turned and kissed her — and Daphne didn't stop him.

When Metal Head put me down, I saw that Scrappy was tied in a corner, still squirming. I looked to find Scooby and located him pulling open a metal hatch in the floor.

He reached down and seemed to be helping someone to climb up. It was Mondavarious — the real one.

I rushed to Scooby's side to see what this was about. "Oh, thank goodness," Mondavarious said. He was very dirty and smelly, but he seemed to be okay. "Two years ago the little pest, Scrappy, arrived at a casting session for our evil elves. Next thing I know, I'm stuck in a black hole and he's out cavorting in a mechanical version of me. Flattering? Yes. But rude!"

Scooby caught sight of Shaggy walking toward him. "Raggy!" he shouted happily. "Raggy! Raggy!" Scooby jumped on Shaggy, knocking him down and licking his face. Shaggy laughed and told Scooby to stop, but I could see he was loving it.

Mary Jane came along and crouched down next to them. The demon was gone and she was back to normal. "Hey, thanks for saving me," she said.

"Like, no problem," Shaggy replied, smiling at her.

Mary Jane looked at Scooby and sneezed. She petted Scooby's head. "And thank you, too, Scooby." She grabbed his cheeks and rubbed them. "What a good little schnookem-wookem."

Scooby was in heaven! I could tell the three of them would get along just great from now on.

FRED

It looked like I was back on top, right where I'd wanted to be. Reporters crowded together outside the Spooky Island hotel. All the college kids clapped and shouted as the gang and I walked out. They shoved autograph books in our faces, which we happily signed. One macho kind of guy even asked Velma to sign his chest. She loved it!

Behind us came Mary Jane, the real Mondavarious, the Voodoo Maestro, and Metal Head. They high-fived the crowd.

Then the police walked out, carrying that little rat Scrappy in a dog carrier. They had Zarkos, N'goo, and all the henchmen in handcuffs.

A reporter stuck a microphone in front of me. "Fred, can you tell us how you solved the case?" she asked.

"It all started when I was giving a speech on

my new book and . . ." I paused, thinking. That was the old Fred talking. Hadn't I learned anything at all?

Yes, I had!

"And I think, really, that the Velmster should take it from here," I concluded. I felt good. Did this mean I'd learned to share the glory? I was trying, anyway.

Velma smiled at me and stepped up to the microphone. "Through the combined intuitive powers of Fred Jones, Daphne Blake, Shaggy Rogers, Scooby-Doo, and myself, we've discovered the villain behind this mystery is Cornelius 'Scrappy' Doo. He attempted to use the power of the Daemon Ritus to rule the world."

"They kicked me out of the group!" Scrappy screamed from inside his carrying case.

Shaggy knelt to speak to him. "Gee, Scrap, that's no reason to freak out like a jerk and destroy humanity," he said.

Scrappy just glared at him. "I would have gotten away with it, too, if not for you meddling . . ." His voice trailed off as the police officer took him away toward the police car.

"Will the demons be coming back?" a reporter asked.

"No," Daphne answered her. "The only way

155

the demons can be summoned is through the Daemon Ritus."

A tall guy with short hair, a suit, and sunglasses approached Daphne. He was some sort of U.S. government agent. Daphne handed him the Daemon Ritus, which was now encased in a clear, Plexiglas box.

Daphne turned back to speak in the microphone. "We've sealed it in this Plexiglas container, which will be safely on display at the Smithsonian Institute," she explained.

Mondavarious stepped up to the microphone and began to speak. "I'd like to thank Mystery, Inc. for saving life as we know it — and, even more importantly, my beloved Spooky Island."

The crowd cheered and we waved to them happily.

Another reporter had a question we weren't prepared for. "Now that Mystery, Inc. is back together, do you have any comment on the Mud Bog Ghoul who's been terrorizing London?"

We froze, then looked at one another, wondering. *Were* we back together? Was that true?

Shaggy was the first to answer. "I've discussed this with my teammates," he fibbed. "He's probably a man in a mask."

Wow! Shaggy had changed! For all these

years he'd believed all the ghosts and ghouls were real. Now he'd finally taken on my rational way of looking at cases.

But I'd changed, too! "But he could be an alien life-form animating an organic dirtlike substance." Did this mean I'd become open-minded?

"Or he could be the ghost of a departed soul who has a disturbing fondness for English soil," Velma added. Supersensible Velma thought it might be a ghost? She'd changed, too.

"Maybe he's not even mud," Daphne put in. "Maybe he's made of goo." Fastidious Daphne would never even have wanted to think about goo before this.

"Whatever the case, Mystery, Inc. will be there," I told the reporters. I put my hand out.

Shaggy put his on top of it. "We'll be solving, like, mysteries."

"Righting wrongs," Daphne added as she placed her hand on top of Shaggy's and mine.

"Squashed together in the front seat!" Velma said, adding her hand to the pile.

And then we heard from the one member of the gang who hadn't changed — who might never, ever change. Thank goodness!

"Rooby-Dooby-Doo!" Scooby cheered.